"FOOD FIGHT!" SOMEONE YELLED.

Aaron rushed into the cafeteria, worried that the students and faculty were being harmed in some way—

And got a face full of mashed potatoes for his efforts.

Aaron shook his head, clearing the food away, and got a good look at the oddball collection of dinosaurs who were scampering across the lunchroom, heaving containers of milk and trays filled with spaghetti or mashed potatoes or mushy brownie-like sludge at one another.

They were all meat-eaters, all tough-looking.

And they were all having an honest-to-goodness food fight!

Long before the universe was ours... it was theirs!

Read all the
DINOVERSE adventures
by Scott Ciencin

DINOVERSE

DINOSAURS
ATE MY HOMEWORK

by Scott Ciencin

illustrated by Mike Fredericks

Random House New York

To my beloved wife, Denise,
for her amazing insights, loving support,
and constant inspiration.
—S.C.

• A NOTE FROM THE AUTHOR •

Dear Reader,

Welcome to Book #6 of DINOVERSE!

If you've read the first five books in this series, you've already seen Bertram Phillips's weird science fair project in action. The device zapped the minds of Bertram and three other Wetherford Junior High students back in time and into the bodies of dinosaurs.

Bertram and his friends had some wild adventures before returning to the present. But the story was far from over. Bertram's science teacher, Mr. London, found a way to make the M.I.N.D. Machine work again. Now Bertram and twenty-nine other students are trapped in prehistoric California, and the fates of two worlds depend on their actions.

Facing fiery volcanoes, lakes of acid, and fearsome predators, Bertram is forced to rely on one of the baddest predators he knows—fellow student J.D. "Judgment Day" Harms.

Will J.D. help Bertram save the future—or will he destroy it?

You may wonder if the age of dinosaurs was anything like what you're reading about in the DINOVERSE books. According to the fossil record, it very likely was. How did the dinosaurs live? What did they eat? What about the weather and landscape? All of those questions have crossed the minds of scientists. And the fossil record has given the answers to them, to me, and now to *you*.

So come back with me to a time when the world belonged not to humans but to the most magnificent creatures the Earth has ever known.

Scott Ciencin

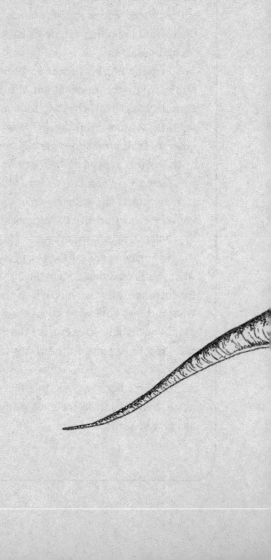

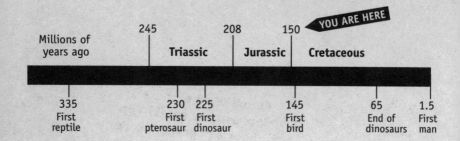

Millions of years ago

245 208 150 YOU ARE HERE

Triassic **Jurassic** **Cretaceous**

335
First
reptile

230
First
pterosaur

225
First
dinosaur

145
First
bird

65
End of
dinosaurs

1.5
First
man

Beverly Hills, California
150 million years ago

Aaron Aimes trudged through the rain and darkness. The scales of his nineteen-foot-long Dilophosaurus body were clammy. The ridges above his forehead were itching and twitching.

The way ahead was lit only by an occasional reddish flash from the volcanoes in the distance and a few silver streaks of moonlight breaking through the ash-covered sky.

Aaron was trying to get back to camp with his companions—a hulking predator with scissor-like jaws and a group of small, vulnerable-looking dinosaurs. But there was one problem: They were completely lost.

When they came to a fork in the path they had been following, Aaron looked back to Holly, or at least to the giant, meat-eating Carcharodontosaurus

1

that now held Holly's consciousness.

She shrugged. Holly had no idea which way to go, either. Her massive scissor-shaped jaws opened and closed. Aaron heard a grunt on the air, but in his mind he heard Holly's voice say, "Up to you, Aaron. You decide."

Aaron nodded but said nothing about not having a clue which way would get them back to camp. That's where they'd find the rest of the Wetherford Junior High students who had been trapped back here in the Age of *Really* Unpredictable Stuff.

Aaron kept his worries to himself because he didn't want to upset the "little guys." These were the four seventh-graders—Jenny, Christine, Joey, and Marv—who were now occupying the bodies of the four small young dinosaurs clustered around his feet.

These four were the reason that Aaron and Holly were lost at all. They had run away from camp when a group of predators attacked. The students back at camp were able to defend themselves and drive off the predators, but these four had already bolted. So Aaron and Holly had been sent into the wilds to find them.

Now the little seventh-grade dinos were looking to Aaron for guidance.

Aaron decided to take the right-hand path. No great intellectual reason, really. He just *guessed*, the way he would have if he had been exploring some new video game back home.

The little quartet chattered excitedly among themselves as they continued their hiking. Aaron was glad they were no longer afraid. He didn't want them to be scared anymore, and he believed Holly would keep them safe from any threat. Now, if only he could find the path that would take them back to camp—

Whack!

Aaron recoiled from the stone that had leaped out of nowhere and sucker-punched him.

"Hey, what's goin' on?" Jenny asked from inside the body of a chicken-sized Compsognathus. "This isn't the way back."

Aaron turned and something smacked him in the forehead. It felt like a small pebble.

"What in the world?" he muttered.

Then, all at once, the rain turned to hail. It struck at them with a strength and fury that sent Aaron reeling.

"Ow!" chirped Christine, in the body of another compie.

"It hurts!" Jenny cried.

Aaron saw the four little guys darting all around as if they could avoid the pelting hail.

They panicked and went running before, Aaron thought. He had to find some way to keep them calm.

Holly surged forward with a roar. "Everybody come here. We have to stay together!"

Lowering her enormous body to a crouch, Holly rolled onto one side. "Use me as shelter. Come on!"

Aaron did his best to ignore the stinging pain of the hail as he shooed the four younger students toward Holly's belly. The hail was falling at an angle, hitting her back full on, but the others were protected.

"Are you okay?" Aaron asked.

"I could be home taking a final," Holly said. "This hurts a lot less."

Smiling, Aaron got all four of the little guys into place. They huddled close, shivering and panting.

"Hey, what if she falls asleep and rolls over on us?" said Marv. He was in the body of a four-foot-long salamander-like Hypsilophodon. "We'll get squished!"

Holly let out a huge, exaggerated yawn and made her belly rumble and quiver against them. Aaron thought it felt like being buffeted by a big balloon. Christine and Jenny chittered with giggles.

"Well, she *could*," Marv grumbled. His buddy Joey laughed along with the girls, wagging his Lesothosaurus tail.

Joey reminded Aaron of Kermit the Frog and sounded kind of like him, too—although Aaron suspected this kid sounded like that even when he wasn't inhabiting the body of a three-foot-long bird-hipped plant-eater.

Aaron looked over at Holly, who stared back with a relaxed and confident look despite the pounding she was taking from the hail.

"I guess we're here for the night," Aaron said.

"Looks like it," Holly said.

Marv snuggled closer to Holly. "Gee, Mom, tell us a story."

Jenny smacked him in the shoulder.

"Ow!" Marv said. "What'd I do?"

"You're such a jerk," Jenny said.

"And a wuss," Joey added. "Can't forget that."

"He won't let us," Christine said.

The four spent a good hour dissing each other, then finally fell into a deep, restful sleep. The hail was still pounding away.

"Are you all right?" Aaron asked.

Holly nodded. "Just worried about what's happening at camp."

A sharp crack sounded from behind them. A heavy tree limb snapped off a hundred-foot-tall araucaria and was blown along the path they had taken. It leaped up and smashed against Holly's head, exploding into splinters. Holly barely seemed to notice.

Whoa, thought Aaron. *Here's a young woman who desperately needs some distraction.*

He looked to Holly. "You know, you remind me of someone."

Holly tensed. Pressed up against her belly, Aaron could feel her muscles grow tight.

"What's the matter?" Aaron asked.

Holly's breathing had become sharp and quick. "Who is it I remind you of?"

"Just a girl I knew," Aaron said. "When I was little, back on the army base when my dad and I lived in Hawaii. She was cool. Really knew what she wanted. And she was strong. You know, on the inside. Like you."

Holly's entire body relaxed. Aaron wondered why the subject had made her tense in the first place.

"This place kind of reminds me of Hawaii," Aaron said. "The volcanoes, being cut off from everyone else. The bugs..."

He swatted a dragonfly the size of his fist, then flicked with his claws at roaches and other little creepy-crawlies who were on Holly's belly and making their way onto the little guys. *Yuck.*

"What do you mean, cut off?" Holly asked.

"Well, I hardly ever saw any of the native kids, just other army brats like me," Aaron explained. "They'd just lock us down and that'd be it. Of course, we'd sneak out."

Holly nodded and looked away, her brow furrowing. Aaron figured that she was thinking about the others—the friends they'd left back at the camp.

"I'm sure everyone's okay," Aaron said. But, in truth, he wasn't so sure.

Bertram, the smartest of their group, had been pushing everyone to their limits. He had ordered them to move his huge, *heavy* M.I.N.D. Machine—the very device that had zapped them all back here. The device that had come with them and appeared to be broken as well.

Anyway, with all the volcanic activity, it was pretty obvious that the place where they had camped would soon be overrun by lava. Bertram had ordered the kids to move the M.I.N.D. Machine and their supplies to higher ground.

Tempers had been flaring, and J.D.—a mean bully of a guy back at Wetherford—had been acting totally weird. Aaron didn't know why, but J.D. was now putting on quite a show, pretending he was all caring and considerate and wanted only what was good for all the kids.

But Aaron got the feeling J.D.'s little act wasn't going to amount to anything remotely good for anyone but J.D.

"I hope it's okay," Holly said. "It's just—"

She stopped suddenly. Her nostrils flared. Her head tilted upward.

Aaron followed her gaze. A burst of crimson from a distant volcano lit the hillside in front of them and allowed him to see a cave opening ahead.

Figures exactly his size and shape scurried near that opening. Predatory dinosaurs that hissed and backed away from the pelting hail. Growls and the sharp, high whispers of slashing claws ripping empty air drifted toward him.

He and Bertram were both in the bodies of Dilophosaurs, and their dinosaur hosts were brothers. Until then, it hadn't occurred to Aaron to wonder where the rest of their Dilophosaurus family may have been.

Now he had the uneasy feeling that he had just seen them.

PART ONE

DAY OF THE

DILOPHOSAURUS

CHAPTER 1

J.D.

J.D. Harms stood in a golden shaft of sunlight that broke through the clouds and the ash-blackened sky. He felt *fantastic*.

The rains had stopped a few hours before, and all the other dinosaurs were fast asleep. They were so exhausted from their work and then the storm that the steady rumble of the spitting volcanoes in the distance was little more than background noise to them.

J.D. left the warming pool of light and walked through the camp. He felt as confident and in control of his brontosaurus body as he did of everything around him.

His new existence was nothing like his life back home. At Wetherford Junior High, the other students viewed him as an angry force of nature to be avoided at all costs. And he had liked it that way.

But here everyone looked to him for guidance. They saw him as the final word.

They *belonged* to him.

J.D. had dreamed of one day being in control of his own destiny, but he had never guessed how good it would feel. Nor had he ever thought that he would be in control of the destinies of others.

What a *rush*!

J.D. walked to the edge of the wide plain where the group had been hauling food and other supplies for the long siege to come. Looking down the side of the mountain, he saw the wreckage of Bertram Phillips's M.I.N.D. Machine—and Bertram himself, in his Dilophosaurus body, sleeping beside the ruined contraption, his arms around it as if it still had the power to make his dreams a reality.

What J.D. had gained had come at a cost—but not to him.

It was Bertram who had paid the price of J.D.'s new leadership status. Looking down at Bertram, J.D. could *almost* feel sorry for the little jerk. But not quite.

There was only one loose end, and that would be taken care of when the lava washed over the machine and the litter that had been carrying it.

Heavy footfalls alerted J.D. to the approach of two Stegosaurs, one from each side of him. J.D. didn't flinch as the ponderous spike-tailed tanks drew up beside him.

"'Sup?" asked Fred Durkovich, also known as "the

Durk" and "Durk the Jerk" and several other nastier names back home. In his strong *new* Stegosaurus form, no one was calling him anything even remotely cruel. Considering the way he was wielding his new-found power and his deadly tail, that was a good thing.

Fred's buddy, Manley Charles Waid, scraped his heavy tail along the ground in a similarly menacing manner. At Wetherford he was known to just about break into tears at the sound of "Manley Man" and "Waid the Maid" or other taunts. He had also done a complete one-eighty after being dropped in the body of a steggie.

J.D. thought they were bigger losers now than ever before. A little power, a little strength, and it had turned them into exactly the kind of bullies they had spent their lives hating.

But they had their uses.

"Checkin' out the loser?" Manley asked. "I think we should send him packing. He knows so much about dinosaurs and stuff, let him go take care of himself."

"I thought you guys were into his whole trip," J.D. said. "You used to read his stories in that magazine and tell him how cool he was."

"That was when they were just stories," Fred said. "How were we supposed to know the time machine was real? And that it was just waiting to nail us?

We're stuck back here, and it's *his* fault."

Manley nodded toward the twisted metal frame and busted-up monitors and circuitry that made up the M.I.N.D. Machine. "I feel like givin' him a wake-up call by smashin' up what's left of that thing."

J.D. disguised his concern. He didn't want anyone poking around in the remains of the machine. The vine that he had nicked to the point of breaking was sitting right there, evidence of the way he had betrayed them all. J.D. couldn't do anything about it without drawing attention. He wasn't worried about shell-shocked Bertram catching on, but he wanted to keep everyone else away from it.

"Deep breath, fellas," J.D. said. "We've got a lot to do today. I don't see the sense in wasting our energy worrying about the past. We've got the rest of our lives ahead of us—provided we don't starve while we're up here waiting for the lava flow to end. We've gotta keep stocking up. The future will take care of itself."

"Yeah, that's right," Manley said.

"J.D.'s the man with the plan," Fred added.

They high-fived with their tails, creating a loud crack that rippled through the camp and woke most of the other students with a start.

J.D. sighed inwardly. *Pathetic,* he thought. A small laugh caught his attention. J.D. saw Melissa watching them. He nodded and she turned away quickly.

Strange. Had she seen the exchange about the machine? Would she become a problem?

"We're gonna get some breakfast, then work on gathering more leaves for later," Fred said. He had made a statement, but his tone was uncertain. J.D. realized he was asking permission.

He loved it!

J.D. nodded. "Sounds like you guys have your priorities straight."

The steggies raised their heads proudly and wandered down the trail along the side of the mountain, stomping close enough to Bertram to make the ground shake. He had to grab at some rocks to keep from sliding. Then he looked to the machine and up at J.D. and hung his head in shame.

J.D. knew that he should have been elated by Bertram's reaction. Instead, he felt nothing at all.

"Yo, J.D.-osaurus!" yelled a loud, unwelcome voice.

J.D. turned to see Reggie Firth. His red hair and trademark football jersey were gone, replaced by the domed head and rocky skull frill of a head-butting Pachycephalosaurus. But somehow his swagger was still the same.

"So, I was thinking," Reggie said. "Now that Bertramus Maximus has been dethroned, maybe we should make this a party day."

"You were thinking," J.D. said darkly.

"A party-hardy day. Lots of music. Fun. Great idea, huh?"

"I still can't get over that you were thinking."

Reggie laughed. He laughed hysterically until everyone was staring at him.

"See?" Reggie said softly. "You're not the only one who can get their attention. So, a party, what do you say?"

J.D. opened his mouth and was about to speak when Reggie cut him off.

"I mean, *I* know what they'll say," Reggie added with a smirk. "So, see, I'm not really asking you, I'm telling you."

J.D. couldn't believe this. He hadn't even had breakfast yet, and already someone was challenging him. Well, he knew how to respond to a challenge. J.D. was just about to rise up on his hind legs and pummel Reggie when Melissa stepped between them. She was in the body of a Massospondylus, a mini long-neck, and she looked as if she had something on her mind.

"Did I just hear you say something about a party?" Melissa asked.

Reggie angled his head a little to one side. "Well, yeah, a party, 'cause—"

Melissa turned to the two dozen other students trapped in the bodies of dinosaurs.

"Hey, isn't that great?" she said. "Holly and Aaron

didn't come back last night, neither did the run-aways, the volcano's gonna blow anytime now, and Cueball Head over here thinks we should have a party."

Everyone stared.

Bobby Giovanni, who was in the body of a long-armed, sharp-clawed Microvenator, laughed. "Hey, yeah, a party!"

Reggie swore under his breath. J.D. looked around. Bobby wasn't the brightest bulb on the porch. Having him agree to the party was about the worst thing that could have happened to Reggie.

"Cueball Head, I like that," said a guy in the body of a Syntarsus.

"Yeah, good one, Cueball Head!" a Maiasaura said. "We'll throw a party when you get lost, too!"

Reggie turned. "Listen, that Cueball thing isn't funny! I was just—"

A chant of *Cueball, Cueball, Cueball* sounded. Reggie stormed off.

Everyone else wandered over to the food supplies and started finding something to eat.

J.D.'s heart was racing. He was ready to go, eager to beat some sense into that jerk Reggie.

"Deep breath," Melissa said. "That's what you told Fred and Manley. I heard you. You handled that really well. That's why I came to your rescue with Reggie. I was impressed."

J.D. took a deep breath—and let it out. His shoulders slumped as the anger eased from him. "Yeah, he's something, all right."

"Believe me, I grok how upset you are," she said. "I know from firsthand experience how Reggie can push anyone's buttons."

"Grok?"

"Grok. It means 'I get it,'" Melissa said. "It's just another way of saying I understand. I read it in a book. *Stranger in a Strange Land*. Science fiction."

"Oh," J.D. said. "I like Faulkner and Hemingway."

"Cool!"

J.D. wondered why he had just shared something personal like that with someone he barely knew. He steeled himself, waiting for her to make some smart remark about Judgment Day Harms actually reading a book.

Melissa shook her head. "I like them. Somerset Maugham and F. Scott Fitzgerald are good, too. And G.K. Chesterton's really funny."

He knew those authors!

"Yeah," J.D. said. "Gatsby. Father Brown. All that stuff. It's good."

Melissa changed gears suddenly. "Listen, Reggie gets to me, too. You just have to know what gets to *him*, then you're okay."

J.D. nodded. He knew that he could have been ticked off at Melissa for getting in the middle of his situation—but instead, he was grateful.

He'd be finished in a second if everyone realized that he was still the same old J.D. and this whole Mr. Compassion thing was just an act.

"I'm worried about Holly and Aaron," Melissa said. "They should have been back by now."

"Um, yeah...," J.D. said. He looked down the hill at Bertram, who sat alone and despondent, and tried to figure out what *he* would say. He raised his chin.

"Maybe they're still looking for the runaways. You know Holly can take care of herself."

"But there were three scissor-jaws out there."

J.D. nodded again. Melissa had a point. He had wanted his two biggest problem cases out of the way when he made his play for control last night. The four brats running off was a perfect excuse for getting rid of both of them.

He hadn't considered that tough-talking "Holly"—who was really "Crystal" Claire DeLacey in disguise—might not make it back at all.

And he needed her. There were predators out there. Big ones. Nasty ones. He needed at least one major terror like her on his side for protection. The whole *group* needed her, really.

Melissa leaned in and talked softly. "The problem is, if they ran into something bad out there, they might need our help. But who do we send? Fred and Manley? They talk tough, but they'd probably faint if they were all alone against something like the scissor-jaws. At least, when they're with the group, they can *act* tough."

"And even if we could, sending them would leave the group defenseless if a threat headed our way," J.D. replied.

"Yeah. So what do we do?"

J.D. didn't have a clue. But he knew he'd have to get one soon. He looked down at Bertram, then quickly looked away. No *way* was he going to go crawling to Bertram for help. He'd never be able to maintain control if he did something as weak as that.

Suddenly, Melissa nuzzled him. He was too startled to draw away, or even to react. He just kept still.

"I know you've got to be feeling bad about last night," Melissa said. "But you did the right thing. Nobody blames you. Bertram brought it all on himself."

J.D. was astonished at what he was hearing. She thought he felt *bad* about last night? This was classic!

Suddenly, J.D. heard shouts from below. He pulled away from Melissa and looked down the mountainside.

Fred and Manley were thundering back up the mountainside, slipping and sliding and beating their tails frantically.

"They're coming!" Fred yelled. "They're coming!"

J.D. looked beyond the panicked pair of Stegosaurus to the shore. Aaron and "Holly" were racing toward the base of the mountain, Aaron with a compie tucked under each arm, "Holly" with the Hypsilophodon clutched in her arms and the Lesothosaurus lightly but firmly cradled in her maw.

The scene might have been funny—if not for the entire *pack* of Dilophosaurs that were on their tails and following them right back to camp!

CHAPTER 2

CLAIRE

Claire DeLacey was in the body of a Carcharodontosaurus, pretending to be Holly Cronk. Why? Because Holly was strong. Holly was powerful. And Holly wasn't back here, as far as Claire knew.

Tired of being "Crystal" Claire, the delicate, fragile one back at Wetherford, she'd decided to make the most of her new hulking, powerful form. No one would respect her if she told them that Claire DeLacey was inside this body—so she'd lied.

She told Aaron and everyone else that she was Holly, the tough chick back at school. She'd disguised her voice, and *voilà*! Everyone bought it. And no wonder. Claire had been a professional actress for years now.

Other than acting the part of Holly, however, Claire really had no idea what she was doing. When the storm had cleared and the way ahead had been a little easier to find, she and Aaron had quickly and quietly gathered up the runaways and tried to slip away without making any noise. They left the Dilophosaurus pack still snoring away in the cave thirty feet above.

After traveling a few miles with no sign that they were being pursued, Claire started to relax. Then the wind suddenly shifted. It had been with them until that point, carrying their scents ahead and away from the predators. Then it had changed direction without warning, and soon the growls and hisses of the pack could be heard.

They had reached the shore before the pack had gotten close enough to be seen. Ahead, Fred and Manley had appeared, chowing down on some seaweed. Claire thought they would be safe. She and the spike-tails would make a stand, and the Dilophosaurus pack would retreat.

Instead, Fred had yelled, "Wauuugghhh!" and ran, his buddy right behind him.

Perfect.

"You fight 'em! You fight 'em!" Manley yelped between gasps as he waddled up the mountainside. "You're bigger than they are!"

Fred and Manley were also bigger than the predators. But that wasn't the point. Facing down the scissor-jaws had been one thing to Claire. But her instincts told her that predators this size could swarm her and wear her down with cut after cut from their razor-sharp claws.

She started climbing, and relief flooded through her as she saw Bertram on a rise above, stumbling to his feet.

"Air support!" Aaron called. "Bertram, you've got the higher ground—we could use some help here!"

But Bertram just stood there. Then she saw what he stood beside. The sight of the ruined M.I.N.D. Machine almost made her falter. Then she heard the growls and hisses of her pursuers and leaped higher and faster to get away from them. Aaron quickly fell behind.

She reached Bertram and dropped the two squirming, crying runaways she carried.

"Bertram, take care of them!" Claire hollered. Then she turned to see two dozen Dilophosaurs swarming up the mountainside.

Aaron was nearly falling over his feet as he tried to run with the squealing compies under his arms. "Bertram, they're Dilophosaurs, like us! How do we make them stop?"

Bertram was still and silent, Marv and Joey quivering as they clung to his legs. Then, suddenly, a thunderous pounding came from behind. Claire turned just in time to see Fred and Manley sliding and flopping back down the mountain, their tails whipping frantically, smashing rocks and sending clouds of dirt into the air.

"We're gonna die, we're gonna die!" Manley whined.

Fred agreed with a shrill shriek.

Far below, the pack stopped and watched in amazement as dinner was delivered right to their door. Claire took advantage of their distraction and raced down to Aaron. She took the compies from him and bolted back to Bertram, handing them over. He still looked dazed, but she was certain he'd snap out of it when the time came. Then she shifted her gaze toward the ledge above, where J.D. and all the others were gathered.

Something was going on up there. J.D. and Melissa were barking orders, and the others were grabbing stuff.

"Holly, buy us a little time!" Melissa yelled.

"Fred! Manley!" J.D. cried. "Show 'em you're not scared! We're counting on you!"

Claire looked back to see Fred and Manley slide right into the center of the first group of Dilophosaurs.

"Use your tails!" Aaron hollered.

Fred and Manley got to their feet and started swinging their spiked tails in wide, frantic arcs.

Whoosh!

Both had to duck. They nearly hit each other! But the Dilophosaurs scattered, avoiding the three-foot-long spikes.

Claire found the biggest rocks around and started kicking them like soccer balls at the predators. The Dilophosaurs scattered under the onslaught but quickly came together the moment she paused to find more stones.

And below, Fred and Manley were getting a little more brave. They stalked toward the predators, stomping their feet and smashing their tails into the earth.

"You want some of this?" Manley taunted. "You want some? I'm right here if you want—"

His statement was cut short as one of the Dilophosaurs leaped at him, slashing at his flank. Manley's howl of pain was high and piercing. The diamond-shaped plates lining his back quivered. Two more Dilophosaurs evaded his flailing tail and sprang at him.

Fred turned tail and ran.

Aaron ran toward them, yanking and kicking and biting at the attacking Dilophosaurs. But they were all bigger than he was and brushed him off as if he was nothing.

"That's it," Claire said. She put her head down and ran with thunderous footsteps toward the predators, roaring at the top of her lungs.

Back home she was "Crystal" Claire. *Don't drop her or she'll break!*

But last night she had faced off against three of the meanest, most terrifying creatures she'd ever imagined, and she'd made sure they would never hurt her or her friends again.

Sure, these guys could swarm her—*if* they got the chance.

She ran to Manley and nearly got nailed by his tail.

"Chill with the tail!" she demanded.

He froze in place. The dilos looked up and let out little squeals of fear. She snatched up one in her maw, yanked him loose, and hurled him twenty feet toward the shore. He splashed into the water. The other two tried to run. She drop-kicked one and belted the other.

They whimpered and scrambled away on hands and knees. But the rest of the pack gathered to face her.

"You guys are toast," Claire said. "It's up to you if you're gonna be lightly toasted or burned to a crisp."

The dilos stared at her.

"Understand?"

And kept staring.

"No?" Claire pulled back her lips, exposing her huge teeth. "Good!"

She waded into them, her tail slapping from side to side, her maw snapping like a set of chattering teeth from a magic shop, her claws slashing at the predators. A trio leaped at her right flank, and she pivoted, smashing the three across the face with a single blow.

Two more sprang at her left flank, and she took them out with her tail. She stomped, kicked, cracked, and pummeled her opposition, her brain overwhelmed by the mad fury of the battle. She felt *alive*. And not in the least as if she was playing a part.

This was *her* and she was ticked. Plain and simple.

Five of the Dilophosaurs retreated, heading up the hill toward Bertram and the runaways. Claire saw that J.D. and the others were about to send their meat reserves over the edge to bait the others away from Bertram and the little guys.

"No!" Claire hollered.

Everyone froze.

Claire ran at her prey, eyeing rocks along the way. Without breaking stride, she kicked four stones with explosive force into the backs of the dilos. All four went down.

Only one remained. She kicked her last stone—and missed.

"Bertram!" she yelled.

He trembled, looked down at the four quavering dinosaurs clinging to him, and shook them free. He looked as if he was about to launch himself against the predator when a stone sent from *somewhere else* cracked against the dilo's head. The predator snapped back and rolled the entire way down the mountainside to the shore.

Claire saw Fred with his tail wagging in the air.

"Did I get him?" Fred asked. "Did I? It was just like in Bertram's story, y'know, the baseball scene? I finally hit a homer!"

Claire saw the rest of the Dilophosaurs limping down the hill. Two of them passed the wounded Manley. He smacked his tail on the ground a few times, and they made a wide circle around him. They picked up their injured family members, helping some to walk, dragging others who moaned and drooled in their semi-conscious state. The moment they were out of view, Manley fainted.

J.D. and the others came down the mountainside. Everyone was cheering and rushing at Claire, calling her Holly.

Only J.D. knew the truth.

"We'll have to post some scouts to make sure we've got some warning if they come back," J.D. said.

He looked to Claire. "We were worried about you guys. What happened with the scissor-jaws?"

The four little guys rushed in and told the tale. Claire tried to correct them on a few basic points, then gave up. Everyone was loving the story the way the kids told it, anyway.

J.D. walked Manley to a stream to clean out his wounds. Back in their time, J.D.'s dad was a doctor, and J.D. knew a lot about the healing arts.

Melissa came up to her. "I swear, girl, you *rule*!"

"Um, thanks," Claire said.

She heard a volcano spitting and churning not far from them. "Look, what happened last night? Why isn't anyone helping Bertram with the machine?"

Melissa's good mood faded instantly. Her gaze narrowed as she peered at the young inventor whose device had brought them all back here.

"You'd better prepare yourself," Melissa said. "There've been some changes around here."

Claire listened to the story of all that had happened while she and Aaron had been away the night before. When it was over, her hope of ever seeing her world again had vanished, to be replaced by the serious need to kick a certain dinosaur from here into the next century.

CHAPTER 3

J.D.

J.D. watched as Claire separated from Melissa and came storming his way. He'd expected trouble from her and was prepared for it.

Sam Mankelvich, the Syntarsus, shook his head. "Wow, that Holly's something, huh? You should hear the little guys talking about the way she kicked the scissor-jaws' butts. With her around, what do we need with you?"

"Go away," J.D. said icily.

"Oh," Sam said. "Right. I'll, ah...I'll get to work."

"You do that."

Sam fled as the earth-shaking predator arrived. But he didn't go far. He turned to watch the confrontation, and so did the other students.

J.D. knew he would have to handle this just right. Claire was still pumped up from her fight, her eyes burning, her nostrils flaring.

Good.

"What'd you do?" Claire bellowed as she halted

31

before him.

J.D. looked up impassively at the towering scissor-jaw. "You want to be more specific?"

"Last night, with Bertram," Claire shouted. "What did you do?"

J.D. craned his long neck in close to her. Softly, he said, "Listen, *Claire*—"

She recoiled as if she'd been struck. She looked around at the students gathered to watch. Nervously, she said, "Keep it down."

"You keep it down," J.D. replied. "I didn't have a lot of fun last night. Fred nearly got throttled. Our only chance of going back home got trashed. And someone needed to tell Bertram the truth. I didn't want to do it, but there wasn't anyone else strong enough."

Claire eyed him suspiciously.

"I wish it had been you," J.D. said. "Maybe you could have figured out a better way of doing it. But you weren't here."

A low growl of frustration came from Claire. Then she bowed her head a little. "No. I wasn't."

"I know I've got a lot to learn about compassion," J.D. said. "What you taught me helped. But no matter how much I teach you, it seems like you think being strong is all about being tough and having muscle. Sorry, but it's not."

Claire looked undecided. "Something feels wrong."

"This whole thing's wrong," J.D. said. "We shouldn't even be here. But we are, and we've got to survive. That's our top priority. Agreed?"

J.D. stared into Claire's eyes. He could feel her intensity waning. His didn't.

She looked away first. "Agreed. I'll take the south-shore watch. I need some time to think."

"Sure," J.D. said. She turned and stomped off.

Suddenly, she stopped and looked back. "Something still feels wrong."

Then she went off down the shore.

J.D. looked at the crowd. "Don't you guys have something to do?"

They instantly dispersed. Fred and Manley approached.

"Yo, boss," Fred said. "We got someone to take the north-shore watch."

"Yeah, that's good," J.D. said. "Who?"

"That slacker, Aaron," Manley said. He raised his spiked tail proudly. "I didn't even have to threaten him or nothin'. He looked like he wanted to do it."

"We don't threaten people," J.D. said. *Man, they're gonna need some rules. More to think about.*

Then Manley's words finally penetrated J.D.'s consciousness. "Aaron?"

"He wanted to be alone," Fred said uncertainly.

"Aaron," J.D. repeated, his thoughts already

whirling. He looked up. "Okay, you guys did good. Thanks."

They walked off, high-fiving their tails again.

Truly sad.

J.D. climbed to the high ground and looked out at the shore. The confrontation with Claire had left him rattled. She wanted time to think. That could be bad. Very bad.

What if she decided to start poking around in the remains of the M.I.N.D. Machine? What if she found out what he had done?

And Aaron...at some point, he was going to have to pay that little dweeb back for getting him in trouble with the faculty at Wetherford. Aaron had messed with him; he had to pay the price. But that guy seemed to be all about getting out of things.

Hmmm...

J.D. knew there had to be a way to take care of the Claire situation. All he had to do was find it.

He looked down at Bertram, who was finally leaving the machine and walking to the shore. He wished he could come up with ideas like Bertram did, but that wasn't his thing. But he'd keep working on it and something would come to him.

It always did.

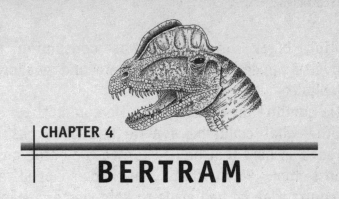

CHAPTER 4

BERTRAM

Bertram Phillips wandered alone by the shore. He felt numb. He didn't want to believe that it was all over, that there was no chance of ever getting home. But the message Will Reilly had sent him from the Dinoverse had told him just what he had to do if there was any hope of saving the future.

Now, with the M.I.N.D. Machine destroyed, Bertram was powerless to reverse the damage he had done when he had thrown himself at Mr. London to stop him from using the M.I.N.D. Machine again. Because of what Bertram had done, the fabric of time and space had been damaged, and the populations of at *least* two worlds were facing extinction.

If he had just believed Mr. London and shown a little faith that the man had truly changed, then everything would have been all right.

He pictured his father in the middle of a lecture with a packed auditorium of journalists and paleontologists, looking up in surprise as one of the rippling black voids that was consuming the Dinoverse appeared out of nowhere and swallowed him whole.

He couldn't let that happen. He couldn't!

But—what could he do? He had been pushing everyone so hard that he had turned the entire group against him. When that vine had snapped and the contraption he had made to help Fred and Manley haul the M.I.N.D. Machine up the mountainside had started strangling Fred, there had been no choice but to cut the remaining vines and let the machine fall to its destruction.

J.D. had made the right call. J.D.'s first thought had been about saving Fred's life. All Bertram had worried about was the fate of his machine.

It was hopeless. *He* was hopeless.

A passage from a book Mr. London had read to him when he had been on the verge of giving up on the science fair came to him: *As long as we have hope, we have direction, the energy to move, and the map to move by. We have a hundred alternatives, a thousand paths, and an infinity of dreams. Hopeful, we are halfway to where we want to go; hopeless, we are lost forever.*

That's how he felt. Lost forever.

The soft crush of sand made him look up. Melissa was coming toward him. The Massospondylus trod softly and with a sense of purpose.

Bertram shrank inwardly. He had failed. The world he knew and the incredible vision that was the Dinoverse would be swallowed whole by a darkness he didn't even understand. And now Melissa was coming to make sure he didn't forget that no matter how much he blamed himself, the others blamed him even more.

Bertram looked around as if he thought he might find a single ally. The excitement over Aaron and Claire's return and the subsequent battle with the dilos had faded, and everyone was back to work, gathering leaves and plant matter, securing fresh water, or casting nets and collecting fish so that they could weather the coming siege.

Reggie was playing deejay again, using his psychic abilities to pump in a steady stream of R&B, ska, and funk music to keep everyone up and moving.

Melissa stopped before him. "How are you doin'?" she asked.

Bertram shrugged. Melissa had stood with J.D. last night. She had been one of his accusers.

"Listen," Melissa said. "I know I'm probably the last person you want to see right now. But the bottom line is that you're not too popular with the others at the moment."

Bertram waited.

Melissa stared at him. Bertram began to feel as if he were in a game of Who Blinks First?

"What do you want me to do?" he asked in a small voice. "Leave?"

Melissa stared at him as if the idea hadn't even occurred to her.

"Sorry," Bertram said.

"It would help if you were doing something. Pitching in. That volcano's going to blow, and we're gonna be in for the duration. The more food we gather now, the less chance there is of tempers getting out of hand and people starting to point fingers when we have to really, really start rationing."

We should be rationing from the beginning, Bertram thought. But he knew the decision wasn't up to him. The group no longer looked to him for leadership.

"Y'know, think of it like that old children's story," Melissa said. "Mother hen, baking the bread? You wanna eat the bread later, you gotta help make it now."

Bertram didn't think he deserved the kindness Melissa was showing him, but he appreciated it.

"We're all going to be together for a really long time," Melissa went on. "We've got to try to get along, right?"

Bertram nodded. "Right."

Suddenly, a voice from above intruded. "Hey, J.D.!"

Fred stood with his spiked tail poised over the

shattered remains of the M.I.N.D. Machine. J.D. was above, looking down from the higher ground.

"We keep trippin' over this junk lying in the path," Fred called as he looked to Bertram. "Mind if we just get rid of it?"

Bertram tensed. He knew it really didn't matter if Fred smashed the machine even more. The fall had wrecked it, and the hail last night had pulverized a lot of the small bits.

Still, the idea of watching it get battered even more made him cringe. He didn't know why exactly. He supposed there was just some part of him that couldn't let go.

"You've got more important things to do," J.D. called back.

Fred's tail sagged in disappointment. He looked away from Bertram and waddled off.

"See what I mean?" Melissa said. "That was just to get a rise out of you. The machine's not in anyone's way."

"Yeah," Bertram said. "They really hate me."

Melissa shrugged. "People can forgive a lot. Look at J.D. The main thing is, you make a change, you mean it, and you let them know you mean it."

A chorus of giggles burst from down the shore, and the music that Reggie was psychically projecting stopped.

"Let's check it out," Melissa suggested.

Bertram walked with her to a small gathering of dinosaurs. They were looking at something they seemed to think was hilarious.

The laughter stopped suddenly as J.D. arrived at the circle at the same moment as Melissa and Bertram. J.D. cleared his throat.

"Mind if I take a peek?" J.D. asked.

Rising from the sand was a five-foot-tall sand sculpture of J.D., the brontosaurus. He wore a great robe like a Roman emperor, but it failed to cover his enormous behind. And his face had the silliest expression Bertram had ever seen on a dinosaur!

In the sand before the sculpture, someone had written BORN TO BE MILD.

J.D. inspected the sculpture, his gaze darting from this ridiculous image of himself to the dinosaurs gathered around. Bertram could feel the growing tension, but he couldn't get a sense of how J.D. was taking this.

"Okay," J.D. said at last. "So, who's the artist?"

Without hesitation, Melissa burst from the crowd, her head bobbing happily. "Me! Ain't it the bomb?"

There were a few small laughs at that.

"Nice try, but I don't think so." J.D. nodded at her hooflike hands. "Not with those."

"Well, it's no biggie, is it?" she asked.

J.D.'s voice was perfectly, frighteningly level. "I

BORN TO BE
MILD

just want to know who did it."

"It was the brats!" Reggie said, pointing at the four younger students.

Someone gave Marv a shove, and he stumbled forward in his little salamander-like body.

"You told!" Marv cried.

"Said I would," Reggie replied.

Jenny the compie chirped and hopped up and down. "But Cueball Head wrote the words, not us!"

"Did not!" Reggie yelped.

"Saw ya!" Jenny shouted. "Cueball Head!"

An amazing thing happened. J.D. laughed. He laughed long and hard, until everyone else was laughing with him. Then he rose up on his hind legs and waved his front paws around to get everyone's attention.

"All right, all right," J.D. said. "We've got a lot to do. Listen, I promise you guys, we'll have plenty of fun and games when this is over. But for right now, we've got to get this work done.

"It may seem like a pain, but when this whole shore is nothing but hot rocks and steam, we're gonna be glad we stored up enough to eat. That's the bottom line. We're not doing this because anyone's telling us to. We're helping ourselves."

Reggie stared at him warily. "That's it?"

J.D. looked to the volcano behind them. It roared and spat fire into the darkened sky. "We don't have a lot of time. When the flow starts, it's gonna wipe out this whole area."

"Yeah, but how do we know that's today?" Reggie demanded. He pointed at Bertram. "We can't go by what *his* buddies are saying. We—"

A sudden splash of water struck Reggie in the face.

"Bleurrrggghhh!" Reggie hollered, spewing and choking.

Bertram looked for the source of the water and

saw a Maiasaura carrying a huge eggshell with the top broken off and water dripping from its top.

Fresh water, of course. They would need plenty of it once the siege began. Four or five other dinosaurs carried similar shells. He'd heard something about them digging a well and keeping it uncovered in case of rain.

Melissa laughed. "That wouldn't have happened if you'd been keeping your big mouth shut, Cueball."

Trembling with rage, Reggie put his head down and raced at J.D.!

The brontosaurus trotted to one side just in time to let Reggie steam past him and crash into the sand sculpture. He fell to the ground, flopping and spewing sand, while the ring of spectators laughed and laughed.

Fred and Manley beat their tails on the sand, making the ground shake. The laughter stopped.

"All right, already," Fred said. "J.D.'s right. You don't have to be a science geek to see how close that thing is to boiling over. None of us are alone in these bodies. What's your inner dinosaur telling you?"

Bertram nodded. The consciousness of his dinosaur host had been pushed down pretty deep, but its instinct for danger had been flaring worse this morning than ever before.

Most of the others seemed to sense it, too. They

hurried back to the shoreline, snatching up what they would need for the siege. Reggie hung his head and joined them. The dejected deejay turned.

"Don't expect any more tunes from me!" Reggie said. His snout twisted into a pout.

A group of dinosaurs whooped and hollered with joy at those words.

"Guy can't even play any country," someone groused.

"Loser," someone else added.

Melissa wandered off with the others. J.D. and Bertram were soon alone with the four *artists*. J.D. pointed at the younger students, who were chasing each other, yelling, "Duckbill, Duckbill, Gigantosaurus!"

"You want to make yourself useful, look after them," J.D. said to Bertram.

"Sure," Bertram replied. He was about to compliment J.D. on how well he had handled the situation when he saw the muscles around J.D.'s dark eyes twitching.

J.D. turned swiftly. "Got stuff to do!"

Bertram watched as J.D. hurried off. He saw Melissa go to him, then get rebuked. J.D. hurried down the shore and quickly out of view.

He looked back to the ruined sand sculpture. J.D. hadn't flown into a rage and smashed it, but it had ended up a ruin anyway.

Just like the M.I.N.D. Machine.

But what had happened last night had been an accident, not something premeditated. If anyone was responsible, it was Bertram. He should have been checking the lines holding the machine for wear, but instead he had just kept pushing everyone.

He looked toward the four younger students, who were laughing and playing just ahead. With a sigh, he went to take his turn at the game of Duckbill, Duckbill, Gigantosaurus.

CHAPTER 5

AARON

Aaron stood alone on the far end of the curving north shore, out of view of the others. The waves gently lapped at his feet as he paced back and forth.

"Okay, so here's the deal," Aaron said, not the least bit self-conscious that he was talking to himself. He was alone so much that it had become second nature to him. "In the plus column, no more rules, no more teachers, no more housekeepers."

Aaron thought about that a little more. "In the super-special bonus-round-plus column, no more housekeepers. I'm tired of being raised by housekeepers and baby-sitters—and Miss Attila the Hun back home was the *worst*."

He took a deep breath and studied the shore. There was no sign of the dilos Holly had driven off. "In the minus column, no more Dad, no more traveling, no more meeting new people, no more pizza, no more PlayStation, no more pay-per-view, no more *Sports Illustrated* swimsuit editions, no more DVDs, no more potato chips, and no more Claire."

An orange fish swam by. Aaron dove in and caught it in his maw, eating it in one bite.

He shuddered. "Add raw fish to the sucky column and put no more Dad and no more Claire in the extra-special *man*-this-is-cruddy column."

Aaron saw a big gray rock sticking out of the water a few dozen yards down the shore. He waded to it and sat down. The tide was getting stronger. Aaron pictured a wave that was twice the size of Wetherford Junior High.

Nature was so out of control in the Jurassic that it seemed all too possible. He closed his eyes and imagined how amazing it would be to surf a curl like that on a bright, sunny afternoon.

A hiss of icy water splashed over him. He opened his eyes, saw the scorched black sky, and stalked out of the water.

"Oh, wait, more to add to the sucky column!" he said. "My personal favorite, *everyone's* walking around wearing I LOVE J.D. T-shirts! It's like, *oh, yeah, I'm still that same guy who used to ram your head into a locker and shake you by your ankles for your change. It's just—well, I've had a hard life, and look, here's my sensitive side.*"

Aaron laughed. "*Right!* I may be the new kid at Wetherford, but I know guys like J.D. Harms, and they don't change."

Then Aaron plopped down on the sand. "So, what am I supposed to do about it? What do I ever do about anything?"

Nothing.

Aaron turned and held his hand out to an imaginary visitor. "Hey, I'm Aaron. What's that you say? You think I'm a slacker? Whoa, no way, dude! I'm just motivationally challenged!"

In the distance, the volcanoes rumbled and hissed as if they were angry at the earth and the sky all at once.

Aaron hung his head. "What can I do?"

He hated feeling helpless. His thoughts went back to the night he was with his mom and they had the accident. They were blindsided on a deserted road after midnight, and their car went up on its side. The other driver took off.

Aaron hadn't done anything to help his mother. She was crying and bleeding and in pain. She was *dying,* and what had he done?

Not a thing.

No one blamed him. He'd been trapped. It had been as though the car's ruined metal chassis had him squeezed in a vise. And he had been knocked around—he was dazed, barely conscious, barely able to breathe.

He didn't tell his mom he loved her. He didn't tell her not to cry.

You couldn't. That's what everyone had told him. But he'd wondered, *Maybe if I'd tried a little harder, struggled a little more, maybe I could have done that much for her.*

No one blamed him. No one expected anything from him. They always made excuses for him, and he accepted that.

But how long could he keep running from things?

A noise and a strange scent drifted from a rocky maze behind him. Aaron rose warily, wondering if the dilos were smart enough to employ ambush tactics.

Hey, we'll just make some noise, lure the dummy into this nice little trap, and bean him. Who needs evolution? Higher intelligence is highly overrated! When it comes right down to it, the old-fashioned, bushwhacking method is always the way to go!

Aaron thought about doubling back and finding help. Then he shuddered and told himself that he had to do this himself. He had to start making a difference.

He approached the rocky crags carefully. Climbing up over a gray hill, he checked for any hint of a trap. The noises were louder now, coming from one of a trio of deep ditches that looked as if they'd been carved with a giant trowel.

Only—his senses weren't warning him of any danger.

Oh, right, brainiac. Like you've got the dinosaur equivalent of spider sense now. You just keep telling

yourself that and step right up. Here we go, a few more steps and we'll get rid of all those nasty little conflicts going on in your pea-sized brain.

Aaron frowned. He was being paranoid. Not everything back here was out to get him. After all, this was Beverly Hills. Home of the stars.

Hi, everyone, I'm Aaron, your tour guide, and hey, look, by the shore there's an oyster bar with two-foot-long oysters, and back at camp, just off Rodeo Drive, there's a movie being filmed, that's why these nutcase dilos are running all over, and this little muddy ditch coming up is the future home of Mann's Chinese Theater, where we'll be telling the same lame-o campfire stories for the next hundred years or whatever our life expectancy is now.

Aaron drew a little closer to the nearest ditch. The pounding was louder now. Aaron's imagination suddenly shifted to something hopeful: He pictured Bertram with a handful of parts from the M.I.N.D. Machine, desperately trying to hammer a new model together.

Was that possible?

Aaron peered over the side of the ditch.

Below, sloshing in the mud, J.D. kicked and pounded at the walls of rock, roaring in a mad fury.

"Okay, actually, this might not be a bad time for the dilo pack to show up," Aaron muttered. "Hey, everyone, look what's for dinner!"

Aaron drew back. He couldn't believe he'd just thought that, let alone said it out loud.

Down in the ditch, J.D. kept kicking and pounding, screaming stuff Aaron couldn't make out. Aaron took that as a sign that J.D. had no idea that he was there or that he had said what he had said.

Good.

Aaron turned to leave, and his foot slid near the edge. He kicked at a heavy stone and got his balance back. The stone dropped and landed with a splat in the muddy ground next to the berserk brontosaurus.

The ruckus in the ditch stopped suddenly.

Aaron tensed and slowly looked back to see the guy who had sworn to kick his butt back in the present staring up at him with dark eyes and wide, flaring nostrils.

"Gee, Aaron, nice to see you, too," J.D. said. "In fact, I was just thinking about you."

CHAPTER 6

J.D.

With slow, measured steps, J.D. walked up the incline, out of the ditch. He kept Aaron in his sights the whole time.

The little weasel looked scared. It was beautiful. Now he could do some real damage.

"What are you thinking?" J.D. asked. "That you know my secret? Whoa, I can still get frustrated and ticked off, just like anyone else. Isn't that a shocker?"

"You don't get angry like everyone else," Aaron said. "When you get angry, things happen."

The slacker was keeping his distance. His muscles were coiled. He was ready to run if it came to that. Not that there was anyplace to run to, but hey, everyone had to have their illusions, right?

"True or false," J.D. said. "I'm the kind of guy who keeps things bottled up, who never tells anyone when he's mad or thinks things aren't going right. I just hang back and go with the flow?"

Aaron didn't answer.

"Let's take that as a given and just say false," J.D. said, taking a few steps toward Aaron—who took a few steps back.

"But right now we're all in trouble and we have to work together," J.D. went on. "The truth is, I don't like it any more than you do. And if I had ended up in the body of one of those scissor-jaws like *Holly*, or even a dilo like you or Bertram, I'd be out of here. I wouldn't care what happens to any of you.

"But that's not the way it is. I can't take care of myself. I found that out the hard way. Coming out here on my own was stupid, but I had to do it. There are too many people depending on my keeping it together right now for me to show them how close I am to losing it completely."

Aaron had angled his head a little to one side. He was listening. Really listening.

J.D. grinned inwardly. He thought of the words of his old friend, the mountain man Trapp. *The beauty of a good lie is to always put just enough truth in it.*

Aaron's brow furrowed. "So you're saying you really care about what happens to everyone?"

"Yeah, for one simple reason," J.D. said. "What happens to you guys happens to *me*. But I can't do anything if you don't believe me. The only thing I can do is ask you to think before you go and tell everyone what you just saw. Because if they don't have someone strong to believe in, someone they think is going to lead them through this—then none of them are going to make it. And Claire's included in that."

J.D. turned and walked away. He made it only a hundred yards when he heard Aaron racing up toward him.

Time for the *coup de grâce*.

"What are you talking about?" Aaron demanded. He circled J.D. and stopped in front of the long-neck. "Claire's back in Wetherford."

J.D. blinked. He looked away—then looked back quickly.

"Claire who? You mean Claire DeLacey? 'Crystal' Claire? I didn't say anything about her."

"Then who did you mean when you said Claire?"

J.D. brushed Aaron aside. "You heard me wrong. I gotta get back. There's still a lot to do."

Aaron leaped in front of him again. "No! Is she here?"

J.D. forced his chest to heave. He made the muscles in his face twitch and he narrowed his gaze. Then he let his shoulders slump and he nodded sourly in defeat.

"The thing is, you've got to promise not to tell her you know," J.D. said. "She swore me to secrecy. I slipped. I'm slipping a lot. I guess I'm just human."

"I swear."

"No," J.D. said. "I've got to know you mean it."

"What do you want me to do?" Aaron asked.

"Claire doesn't want anyone to know she's here," J.D. explained. "She hates the way people treat her. The whole 'Crystal' Claire thing. *Don't drop her, she might break.* If people find out, it's all gonna start up again."

"She told *you* her secret," Aaron said. "You?"

"She said she figured we had a lot in common," J.D. replied. "People take one look at me and think they've got me all figured out. I'm sure *you* don't get that."

Aaron thought about it, then nodded. "All right, look, I won't say a thing. But I've gotta know. It may sound crazy, but there was something between her and me. I could feel it."

J.D. started walking. Aaron kept pace beside him. "She doesn't want anyone acting any differently around her. She wants people to think she's tough and that she can handle herself. I think that's the other reason she came to me."

"Just tell me," Aaron said. "Come on, I'll do anything."

"Really?" J.D. looked to the shore and took a good long time before saying anything else. He wanted to put on a great performance for his new buddy Aaron. Make it look as if he was really thinking this over. Agonizing over it.

"I mean it," Aaron said.

It was just too easy.

"I need someone to stay close to her," J.D. said. "Make sure nothing happens to her. Watch her back. Can you do that?"

"Yeah!"

"Without letting on that you know her secret?"

Aaron nodded like an anxious puppy. J.D. had to struggle to keep himself from bursting into laughter. With Aaron all over her, Claire would be too preoccupied to worry about what had happened last night.

"It's Holly," J.D. said, letting the air out of his lungs with the words. "I can't believe I'm telling you this, but it's her."

"Holly Cronk?" Aaron said. "Yeah, right."

"Claire's an actress," J.D. said. "She's been on TV and everything. You think playing the role of Holly Cronk is that much of a stretch for her? Think about it."

Aaron faltered a little, but J.D. kept moving toward the group now gathered on the shore. Bertram was playing with the runts, and Claire was nowhere to be seen, which meant that she was still guarding the south shore. Aaron quickly caught up.

"Okay," Aaron said. "You got it. But it doesn't mean I trust you. Or that I think for a second that you've really changed."

"Sure," J.D. said. "You think what you *want* to think. Just make sure you don't forget your promise.

Claire—Holly—she's important to all of us. And she's acting like she's got so much to prove. If she isn't careful, I don't know what might happen to her."

"I'm not gonna forget," Aaron said.

"Cool."

He watched Aaron head off, then surveyed the work front. Everyone was doing their jobs, carrying water, gathering fish and greens for the siege. He could never have commanded people like this back home.

He stopped. What a weird way to think of the time he had left behind. *Home.* Like he was gonna miss it. Like anyone except maybe his mom was gonna miss him.

He called to Reggie.

"Hey, Cueball," J.D. said. "Guess who just volunteered to watch the north shore?"

Everyone laughed as Reggie threw down his net and trudged off. He passed J.D. closely enough to brush against him if he so desired but veered off at the last second, out of the bronto's reach.

J.D. trotted happily into the midst of the other students, thinking that all that stuff his old friend Trapp used to tell him was true.

Living well really *was* the best revenge.

CHAPTER 7

CLAIRE

Claire stormed back and forth along the shore. She almost wished the Dilophosaurus pack would return. Anything would be better than being alone with her thoughts.

A school of blue-striped fish came into view. She waded slowly into the water, trying not to make waves, and positioned herself in the path of the fish. She stood perfectly still until they were about to swim by, then gathered as many of the wriggling morsels as she could in her massive maw.

Stomping and splashing back to shore, Claire deposited the food near a huge pile she had already amassed. She hadn't decided exactly how she would get all this food back to the group, but she had to do something to keep busy.

Maybe Bertram could help her figure out a way to get the supplies back to camp.

Bertram. Oh, sure. *He* would be a big help.

The last time she had seen him, he had looked

semi-comatose. Not that she could blame him. What had happened to him—to all of them—was pretty horrible.

She pictured how she would pitch it if she were talking to her agent back home. The conversation played just like a scene from one of the many scripts she read:

Int. CMI Talent Management Office—Day

CLAIRE, in her fragile HUMAN body, sits across from her agent, who eyes her PHONE, where she has two people on hold. Her AGENT is blond, beautiful, and in her forties. A former child star herself whose first job was as a stand-in for Marcia Brady.

AGENT:
Okay, so I'm with you so far. This whole bunch of junior high school students are thrown back in time and into the bodies of dinosaurs. Only one of them, that's you, isn't happy with her life. So she figures, no one knows who I really am in this dino body, I'll just reinvent myself.

CLAIRE:
Right, and I picked Holly Cronk because nobody knows her too well. She's really tough and she keeps to herself. Only the bad guy, J.D., he figures it out

and makes a deal with her. She teaches him how to look like he pretends to care, and he teaches her how to pretend to look tough.

AGENT:

But now she's changing. She's becoming more and more like Holly.

CLAIRE:

Well...mostly. The main thing is, Holly wouldn't care what anyone thinks of her. But it means everything to me. And sometimes, I think I'm feeling strong, I'm acting like I'm strong, but inside I'm still scared. Scared and weak.

AGENT:

Quite the predicament. And the whole thing's worse now because you're trapped in the past forever. And with this J.D. guy, you feel like you did your job too well. He's got everyone conned.

CLAIRE:

Yeah, except—if I can change, why can't he? Maybe he is telling the truth. I'm just all mixed up. I want answers. I want to do the right thing.

AGENT:

Don't we all. Okay, so you're sure there's no way

back. That's not like, a relief, is it? In the past, you can play Holly the rest of your life. Back home, you're "Crystal" Claire again. And if you start acting tough as "Crystal," who's gonna believe it?

Pause. Claire says nothing. She looks out the fortieth-floor window at the L.A. skyline, lost in thought.

CLAIRE:

I wish things could just be simple. Like they are in the Dinoverse.

AGENT:

Refresh my memory about that.

CUT TO flashback sequence. Quick montage of Will Reilly surrounded by hostile, intelligent raptors in a classroom at Wetherford Junior High. He smashes a window and leaps into the swirling void surrounding the school. Then he finds himself in a technologically advanced, peaceful world populated by highly evolved dinosaurs. He sees wondrous architecture and machines that create anything one could wish for. He also sees dangerous black holes that eat through the fabric of this reality.

An inner call drives him to find a scientific laboratory run by a gentle, compassionate brontosaurus who is the Dinoverse's version of J.D. Harms. They create another M.I.N.D. Machine and send a message telling Bertram and the others that they must save themselves and the machine from the imminent eruption of a nearby volcano. The machine must be repaired so that the natural flow of time in a multitude of realities may be restored. If they fail, they will be stranded in the past, and the future—all futures—will be in peril.

CUT back to a CLOSE-UP of the agent.

AGENT:
You call that "simple"? Remind me not to ask you for something complicated!

CUT to—

"Hey, uh...hey, Holly!"

Aaron was coming her way from the direction of camp. *Was there trouble?* She almost hoped there was.

"What is it?" Claire asked.

"Nothin'," Aaron said. He was practically out of breath by the time he reached her. "I just wanted to see how you were doing."

Claire frowned. "How do you *think* I'm doing? I've just been told I'll never see home again. I'm fine."

"Okay. Stupid question."

Aaron looked to the pile of fish she had caught. "You want some help with the fishing expedition? Looks like you're gonna need a bigger boat!"

Claire laughed. She couldn't help herself.

"*Jaws*. I like that movie, too."

Then she sighed. She *liked* Aaron. A lot. He was so uncomplicated. And he could make her laugh. Here or back home.

"You want to talk?" Aaron offered.

"I just keep thinking there's got to be something we can do," Claire said.

"There is. Keep everyone safe and calm and focused on getting through this." Aaron pointed a claw at the bubbling lava peak in the distance. "It's not gonna be long now."

"That's not what I mean." Claire shook her head.

"I know," Aaron said. "None of us wants to be trapped here. But what else can we do?"

Claire went back into the water. Her nostrils flared. "Do you smell that?"

Aaron waded in beside her. "I smell something. Kind of well done. Char-grilled."

"Yeah," Claire said. She took a few steps farther south, then kept walking until she could make out a figure in the distance.

It was one of the two remaining scissor-jaws. The immense dinosaur came running along the shore in their direction. He looked weak and uncoordinated but advanced relentlessly. The roar that came from his maw conveyed more pain than fury.

"We'd better get out of here," Aaron said nervously. "Warn the others."

"I don't think so," Claire replied. For some reason, she didn't feel in the least bit threatened. "You go if you want."

"I'm not leaving you alone to face that."

"Whatever...," Claire said distractedly.

The scissor-jaw advanced, the earth trembling under his thunderous footfalls. Claire felt a connection to the dinosaur. They were both alone and adrift now.

"Holly, come on, you're not Wonder Woman," Aaron cried. "I know the little guys have been doing some good press on you and all, but that thing's a killer."

Claire was beginning to feel annoyed. "I know just what it is. It's the same as me."

"*That?*" Aaron said shrilly. "You've gotta be trippin'. Let's go."

"I told you," Claire said, "*you* go. I want to see what he wants."

"Probably to rip your head off for deep-frying him," Aaron said. "Holly, please!"

She spun around, roaring so loud right in his face that he stumbled back and fell with a splash into the water.

"I'm all right, got it?" she hollered. "What, do I have a sign over my head? *Help me! Save me! Oh, I can't look after myself!*"

Aaron looked over her shoulder, his eyes wide as he fixed on something directly behind her.

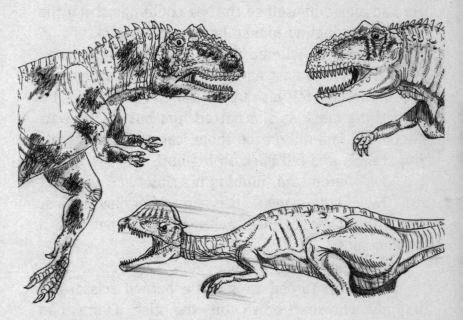

Claire turned to see the burned scissor-jaw only a few feet away. He looked at her hungrily, drool falling from his maw. The huge dinosaur's claws were shaking. His entire body quivered.

Claire knew what he wanted, and she had no problem giving it to him. She stepped out of the water and stood in front of the fish she had collected. The scissor-jaw advanced.

Scrambling free of the water, Aaron yelled something and launched himself at the wounded predator.

"I'm not gonna let it hurt you!" Aaron yelled, his claws flashing.

Claire suddenly knew what Aaron was going to do: He had aimed himself so that he could hamstring the dinosaur, crippling him so he couldn't attack.

"No!" Claire hollered. She surged forward, smacking her snout against Aaron's flank before he reached his victim. She felt a sharp pain in her jaw and heard something crack as she batted him out of the way. He landed in a roll on the shore, came out in a fighting stance, and fell back on his butt.

"Ow," Aaron said, rubbing his ribs.

"Ow," Claire agreed, massaging her jaw against her chest. She opened her maw and spat out a broken tooth.

Munching sounds came.

They both turned to see the burned scissor-jaw happily chowing down on the fish Claire had collected. He looked up suddenly when he saw that they were staring at him, then took a frightened step back.

"Get a mawful of fish," Claire said to Aaron. "I'll do the same. Leave the rest for him."

"I don't know," Aaron said.

"I *do*," Claire said firmly. "So do what I tell you."

Aaron did as he was told. They were half a

mile down the shore when a sound came from behind them. It was a mournful call. A thank-you, possibly. Or a cry of loneliness from the wounded scissor-jaw. Claire didn't look back. She had done all she could do for the dinosaur. Now that he had fed, maybe he would have a fighting chance when the lava flow hit.

They reached the others. A section had been designated for fish drop-offs, and so they dropped the fish they were carrying. Other dinosaurs were gathering up the fish and moving them to higher ground.

Shrill laughter captured Claire's attention. She turned to see Bertram in the water, catching fish, then tossing them to Marv, who passed them to Joey, then to Christine, then to Jenny, who tossed them onto the food pile.

It was good to see Bertram back with the others, and even the students were beginning to look comfortable having him in their midst. That was a good sign.

"Hey, Bertram, can we play hide-and-seek again?" Marv said.

"We've been playing all morning!" Bertram said.

"We like that game!" Jenny said with a slight whine.

"Okay, okay!" Bertram laughed. "Let's take a break and play right now."

"Cool!" the little guys cried. They flew past Claire and Aaron, Bertram right behind them.

Claire waited until they were out of hearing range, then spun on Aaron. "You want to tell me what's going on?"

"Nothing."

"Bull. Get it through your head, the last thing I need is someone protecting me."

"I see that." Aaron threw up his hands. "I dunno, I was just trying to pay back the favor. You saved me from the dilos. You saved all of us. I just wanted to feel like I was good for something. Like there was something I could actually do."

Claire nodded. "Yeah. I wish there was something we could *both* do. But this is it. None of us are going back."

She walked with Aaron toward her station. The wounded scissor-jaw was gone.

"It's not all bad," Aaron said. "Back at home, you wouldn't even take a second look at someone like me. At least here, you talk to me."

"I'm Holly Cronk," Claire said. "I'm a bad, bad girl. As tough as they come. How do you know you're not just my type?"

"'Cause I'm not so tough."

Claire looked back and saw Fred and Manley "jousting" with their tails while a small group of dinosaurs watched.

"Yeah, well, at least you can admit it," Claire said. "There are times when I wish I could just tell everyone—"

An explosion in the distance captured everyone's attention. Claire and Aaron turned to see a reddish yellow stream of steaming lava sliding down the edge of the nearby volcano—it was heading right for them.

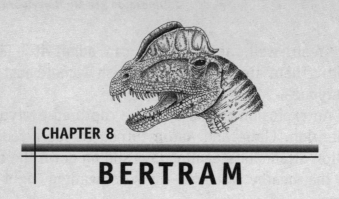

CHAPTER 8

BERTRAM

Bertram heard the explosion and knew at once what was happening. He'd been in the middle of a game of hide-and-seek with Marv and his friends when the signal he'd been dreading came.

"That's it!" J.D. hollered. "Everyone *move*!"

Bertram searched frantically for his charges. He'd call to them and they'd respond, but he could never find them.

"The game's over, come on, we're in trouble!" Bertram hollered.

Marv appeared, then the others. The moment they saw the mountain peak glowing golden and bubbling over with fiery lava, they stopped playing and followed Bertram. He led them to the long line of dinosaurs who were pushing and shoving their way up the incline to the safety of higher ground.

Fred and Manley were blocking the narrow path. The gigantic steggies were moving side by side and had to be separated by Melissa. Marv was so startled by her arrival that he slid and nearly mashed the feet of a Corythosaurus and the Maiasaura who had splashed Reggie earlier that day.

Megan, the Maiasaura, bit his backside and told him to stop acting like a wuss.

Megan helped Melissa guide the steggies into a single file, allowing the swifter and smaller dinosaurs to rush around them.

"It's going to be one of those days," Megan said.

But it didn't look like day, not anymore. The sky was pitch-black, and a soft rain had begun to fall, creating a crimson mist as it struck the flowing lava from the nearby peak.

Manley stumbled off the trail, and a great *crunch* sounded. Even over the roars and volcanic explosions, Bertram heard the distinctive sound of metal twisting and glass breaking.

The machine!

"Stupid thing, I think I hurt my foot!" Manley whined. He raised his tail high.

"Don't!" Bertram yelled.

The spiked tail whipped downward, smashing into the ruined chassis of the M.I.N.D. Machine. Bits of metal and glass flew outward like shrapnel. Bertram saw Marv and Jenny right in the line of fire and leaped in front of them, shielding them with his body. He grunted in pain as something sharp and cold dug into his side.

"That's enough!" J.D. called from the shoreline. "Everyone move!"

Marv pulled back from Bertram with wide eyes. "You're hurt!"

"You're not," Bertram said. "That's what matters."

He ushered Marv and Jenny ahead, doing his best not to look at the wreck of the M.I.N.D. Machine.

Manley glanced over his shoulder at Bertram. "I've been wanting to do that for a while."

Bertram couldn't help but take another look at the machine. He started. Something about it seemed different. He couldn't say *what* exactly. But even with all the damage it had sustained, it didn't look quite the way it should have.

He told himself it was a trick of the light. The lava was flowing down the side of the opposite mountain like melted-down gold, beautiful and terrifying all at once.

Between the wildly streaking rain and the odd hues cast by the volcanic eruption, Bertram couldn't be one hundred percent sure *what* he was seeing.

He soon reached the level ground above, where Joey and Christine were waiting.

"Whoa, this is like something on the Discovery Channel!" Joey said.

Bertram nodded and watched as the lava flowed onto the shore, then to the water beyond. Incredible clouds of steam rose as the water instantly evaporated and the shore turned to steaming black stone.

Then he looked at the twisted path leading down the side of this mountain and couldn't see J.D. He'd been down there just a second before!

A voice rose above the thunderclaps. "Move, you stupid Cueball Head!"

Bertram saw J.D. still on the shore, racing an ever-expanding, bubbling wave of lava with Reggie in front of him. J.D. pounded and kicked at Reggie to get the terrified eighth-grader to stop looking back and move to safety.

"It's so *hot*!" Reggie hollered.

Bertram could feel the blistering heat from where he stood. He saw fingers of flaming lava reach out through the valley. Soon, the mountainside below them would be engulfed.

"Move!" J.D. yelled.

But Reggie wasn't moving—not unless he was given a shove.

Neither of them was going to make it!

A girl screamed as a burning tongue of flame seared J.D.'s tail. Another yelled as the yellow-and-red pools of steaming lava rushed around the pair, filling in small ditches that raced on either side of J.D. and Reggie like a wishbone.

Marv grabbed Bertram's hand. "Do something. Come on, *do* something!"

Jenny joined in. "Bertram, please!"

Bertram was stunned. He looked around at a sea of frightened and expectant faces.

Holly and Aaron surged forward.

"Any ideas?" Aaron asked.

Bertram scanned the horizon. The lava flow raced around in front of J.D. and Reggie, forming a hangman's noose of searing crimson-yellow liquid around them. They were trapped!

Racing down the mountainside, Bertram called, "I'll tell you on the way!"

He took a diagonal path that had rarely been used by the others but that he had noticed on one of his first inspections of the area. His only fear was that Holly or Aaron would miss a step and fall into the gathering darkness. But they stayed with him.

He saw a huge tree near the small island upon which J.D. and Reggie had been marooned.

Behind him, Aaron called to Holly, "Go back! We can handle this!"

"No! We need her!" Bertram yelled, wondering why Aaron had said such a thing.

A roar sounded, Holly's only reply.

They reached the tree and Bertram pointed at it. "Holly, drop that thing like a drawbridge!"

She surged forward, ramming the tree with her shoulder. It cracked and fell, but not the way Bertram had hoped. Instead of landing on the little flat where J.D. and Reggie were trapped, one end fell in the lava.

Before Bertram could say anything, Holly knelt and grabbed hold of the shattered tree trunk. She moved it into position, its flaming head sparking and hissing as it nearly swiped J.D. into the ring of flames.

"Reggie, run across it!" Bertram yelled.

The startled Pachycephalosaurus cringed. Bertram's gaze locked with that of J.D. The brontosaurus raised his chin.

"Come on, Reggie," J.D. said. "You can do it!"

Reggie leaped onto the brittle tree trunk. One end of the huge log was already burning, and a crimson glow was reaching up from its core. It crackled and spat like wood in a fireplace.

With a yelp of pure panic, Reggie raced across the burning tree trunk. Bertram saw the log start to buckle just as Reggie leaped to safety.

"Aaron, get him to the others," Bertram commanded.

The wiry Dilophosaurus looked to Holly and shook his head. "But—"

"Go!"

Aaron grabbed Reggie's arm and hauled the frightened bonehead into a crimson mist and out of sight.

The tree trunk collapsed, leaving J.D. trapped. All around him, the lava flow was mounting. It wouldn't be long before it lapped up over the small rise J.D. stood upon and engulfed him.

J.D. looked around at the mounting tide of lava as if it was an enemy he could face with brute strength alone.

And he was right.

"You know what you have to do," Bertram yelled.

J.D. nodded. "Which way?"

Bertram looked back and up at Holly's watchful

gaze. She stood at nearly three times his height. "He's going to have to jump the fence. Do you understand?"

The scissor-jaw nodded. She retreated a few steps, straining to raise her head as high as she could while surveying the area.

"Toward the shore," she said. "It'll be tight. There's another river of lava he'll have to leap over. But that's the best chance I can see."

J.D. turned his back, got as much of a running start as he could, and leaped into the steaming mist formed by the noose of lava. There was a sharp cry, then nothing.

The rains worsened, and a cloud of steam totally obscured their view. Bertram looked back to Holly, who nodded at a curtain of lava that was surging their way from above.

"We've gotta go!" she yelled. "Now!"

"You first!" Bertram said. "You can see higher and better!"

Holly ran off. Bertram followed her. There was no sign of J.D.

Suddenly, the mists parted, and Bertram thought he saw a figure crossing the shore. He also spied the other obstacle Holly said J.D. would have to face— the artery of lava that was flowing his way.

But Bertram saw one thing more—a deep chasm that had been hidden until then. It was revealed by the light from the rapidly extending line of lava.

J.D. was there—and he was heading right for it!

Drawing a sharp breath, Bertram saw the lava flood coming from above. He raced down the mountainside, leaping over the burning chasm to land on the island J.D. had just deserted.

He thought he heard someone yell his name, but it didn't matter now. He got a running start and flung himself at the wall of rising mist where J.D. had disappeared.

The mist was scalding, and Bertram yelled as the heat seared his scales. Then he was over the lava-filled chasm, scrambling to his feet. He saw J.D. racing ahead and ran to reach the side of the charging brontosaurus.

"J.D.!" Bertram yelled. "Stop! There's a chasm! A pit!"

The brontosaurus didn't hear Bertram over the noise. Bertram ran as fast as he could, circling in front of J.D., then springing up to smash into his flank and bring the sauropod down seconds before he might have spilled into the abyss.

J.D. rolled and got to his feet. Bertram rose and saw the chasm before them filling with lava. It was a good ten feet across.

"There's a narrow spot in from the shore," Bertram said.

"Right," J.D. said.

They ran together, outracing this new obstacle by seconds. The narrow place Bertram had seen had a small dip they could cross, but the lava was flowing in hard and fast.

"Don't stop!" J.D. called.

Bertram didn't. He crossed down into the chasm, seeing the rush of reddish yellow lava bubbling as it flowed below him. J.D. was behind him. They were back on solid ground as the chasm filled and lava spewed over the top, spitting and striking at them.

Bertram and J.D. reached the second hurdle of flames and jumped them together. Then they were racing uphill, past the wreckage of the M.I.N.D. Machine and toward the safety of the high ground, where the other students cheered and called their names.

They clustered around Bertram while Melissa went to J.D. and nuzzled him as the fires and the lava lapped at the earth below.

Bertram turned to see a curtain of lava flow across the path they had just taken. In its bright glow, he saw the lava blanket the M.I.N.D. Machine. The metal chassis and all of its remaining parts hissed and turned to slag as the inferno splattered over it.

"Get back from the edge, everyone!" J.D. yelled. Several students shrieked as they were singed.

Bertram led the younger students away. They found a quiet spot and settled down. The image of the M.I.N.D. Machine melting away stayed in Bertram's thoughts as he watched the lava flow from the nearby volcano and felt the soothing cool rain wash over his burns.

Jenny was the first to speak. "Wanna play a game?"

Bertram looked at her with disbelief. "I don't think I'm up to it."

"It's hide-and-seek," Jenny added. "Only it's easy, 'cause we've already done the hiding, and you don't really do any seeking, 'cause we'll take you right to it."

Bertram was intrigued, and despite his exhaustion, he wanted to experience something that would take his thoughts away from the destruction of their only route home.

"Okay," Bertram said as he forced himself to rise. "Show me."

The shelf of level ground that they had picked for the long siege was connected to even higher hills and caves. Bertram and Marv's buddies quietly slipped into one of these caves to a spot that was illuminated by a shaft of red light penetrating a cavity in the cave's ceiling.

Bertram gasped as he saw what his friends had done. Neatly gathered in the crimson glow were dozens of little circuit boards, a keyboard, and several panels and other bits and pieces of the M.I.N.D. Machine—including one intact monitor.

"No one pays any attention to us," Marv said. "When we were playing hide-and-seek before, we kept seeing how much of this stuff we could grab before someone stopped us. No one even noticed."

"We figured you'd want something to play around with," Joey said. "Maybe you can show us how to make a radio—"

"Or walkie-talkies," Jenny added.

"Yeah," Christine added. "That'd be cool!"

Bertram stared at the collection of odds and ends that the younger students had scavenged. He honestly didn't know which parts of the M.I.N.D. Machine had made it work and which parts were junk. And all things considered, so long as he kept what he was doing quiet so that he didn't raise any false hopes, what harm could it do to play around with the machine a little?

Mr. London's words came to him as forcefully as if the man were standing beside him: *Great works are performed not by strength, but by perseverance.*

"What do you think?" Marv asked.

"Yeah!" Jenny said. "Can we make something out of this?"

"You never know," Bertram replied with a smile. "You never know..."

PART TWO

THE BRONTO
STRIKES BACK

CHAPTER 9

J.D.

The night was alive with fireworks. Burning, spiraling, streaking hunks of rock reached up to tap the clouds in celebration.

J.D. was mesmerized.

When he was little, he and his family lived in New York City, and the Fourth of July was always his favorite holiday. His dad would take them from one borough to another, letting them witness spectacular displays mounted all across the city. Those were good days, uncomplicated days. He still saw his dad as a strong man, a doctor who could take on anything, any illness, any problem, and hold his own.

That had been before the accident. Before J.D. was forced to grow up and really see his dad for what he was.

Standing upon the vast clearing with the others, watching the amazing display put on by the erupting volcano, J.D. thought about the simple times, those days before he had come to despise his father for the man's weakness; the days when his mother's face—now frozen by the many surgeries she had had to endure—could still smile or cry.

"Oh, the hero stands alone, all dark, brooding, and intense," Melissa said.

J.D. craned his long neck to look at the approaching Massospondylus. She stepped beside him, and their flanks brushed against each other. It felt comfortable and right and yet a little strange and troubling at the same time. J.D. had never had a girlfriend before. Dates, girls he fooled around with, sure, but no one like Melissa.

That is, if he was reading her right, and she didn't just want to pal around.

"I'm not brooding. I just think it's pretty."

Whoa, had he actually spoken those words? What was wrong with him?

"Me too," Melissa agreed.

Suddenly, a burst of sobs cut through the night, rising over the deep rumbling and sharp thunderclaps from the volcano. The rains had all but stopped, and mist clung to the ground, carrying with it a dull crimson glow. Smoke and the sharp, bitter smell of flames assaulted his nostrils.

J.D. went with Melissa to a small gathering of young women, four in all. Megan, the Maiasaura, was in the middle. She looked hysterical. She was shaking, and two of the other dinosaurs were holding her, but it wasn't doing any good.

"We're never going back!" Megan shouted. "We're never going to see home. We're going to die here!"

"Stop it," J.D. said sharply.

Melissa looked to him in surprise, and he frowned inwardly. He knew that getting ticked at Megan wasn't going to help the situation, but he didn't want her scaring the others. Megan had been one of the few who had really held it together up until this point. He had to do something.

"We're going to be okay here," J.D. said. "We're going to be better than okay."

Megan sobbed. "How do we know we have enough food? And the water, did anyone cover the water?"

"It's all under control," Melissa said in a gentle, soothing voice. "I've seen to it myself."

"What are we going to do?" Megan shuddered. "How are we going to live our lives? What's it going to be like when we can leave the camp?"

"We've got to concentrate on getting through tonight," J.D. said. "Then we'll get through the next day, and then the next."

That was how he lived his life, especially now, so it seemed like the only reasonable response.

He studied Megan's face and saw that what he was saying wasn't enough. The dinosaurs who had been comforting Megan looked alarmed. Others were coming their way. It wouldn't be long before an all-out panic took place. J.D. couldn't afford that. None of them could.

They needed something familiar to hold on to, he decided. But what?

J.D. took a step back and motioned to Melissa. She followed him to the edge of the plain. They would have to jump back quickly if any lava spat up at them, but it meant only that this was a private place. No one else would come here. And over the noise, probably no one would be able to hear them.

"I don't know what to do," J.D. admitted. It seemed that he could admit anything to Melissa. The words of his old friend Trapp came to him: *Information is ammunition. Don't give it away unless you're sure.*

"They want order," Melissa replied. "They want somebody to make sense out of all this for them, and I think they want something else to think about. We've all had something to do up until now, and I think we were all hoping for some miracle. Somehow, at the last second, it would all turn around and we would get back. Like in Bertram's stories."

"Right," J.D. said. And it was his fault that they weren't. His decision, made for all of them.

"Okay," J.D. said as he turned and stepped away from the edge. In a loud voice he called, "Everybody gather around—we have to talk."

It took only a few moments for the group to assemble in a circle. Melissa stood with J.D.

"I know some of you are scared," J.D. said. "But we *are* safe here and no one's going to starve. We've got food for the plant-eaters and the meat-eaters. We've got fresh water. But we've got to consider that we are going to be up here for a while and there's stuff that needs to be done. Like—someone is going to have to be in charge of the rationing."

There were groans.

"I know," J.D. said. "More work, right? But—"

"I'll do it," Melissa said.

J.D. shook his head. "I need *you* to keep an eye on everything just like you have been doing. Make sure that everything is getting done."

Reggie raised his hand meekly. "I'll do it."

"Oh, great," little Jenny muttered. The compie rolled her eyes. "Cueball Head is going to be in charge. I don't think he can even count."

"Chill with that," J.D. said. "Reggie, there are better uses for your skills. I want you on the entertainment committee."

Reggie's eyes brightened. "There's going to be an *entertainment committee*? Really?"

"Hey, I said there was a lot to do." J.D. laughed. "I didn't say that none of it was going to be any fun."

"Cool," Reggie said. "Thanks."

"Don't mention it," J.D. said. He wondered how

long Reggie would stay humbled by his recent experiences.

"I want parties. I want games. I want karaoke. I want drive-in cinema. Anything that you guys can come up with."

Megan raised her hand. "How about a girls' and a boys' side of the camp? Otherwise, it's just kind of weird."

"Sounds okay to me," J.D. said. "Anyone got any objections?"

There weren't any.

"How about you're in charge of setting that up?" J.D. said.

Megan's mood seemed to brighten. "Okay."

This is working, J.D. thought. "Some of what's going to be needed we can work out on rotating shifts. I'm gonna supervise the rationing. We'll also need perimeter guards. I know we're alone up here, and it doesn't seem likely that anything is going to reach us. But once it's safe to go back to the shore, we're going to need to post guards, so it'll be good to get in the habit now."

"We need a poop patrol," someone yelled. Everyone laughed.

J.D. understood. A couple of areas had been designated as lavatories, but someone had to clean them out from time to time or else the smell would become unbearable.

"Okay," J.D. said. "I think we're going to have to draw lots on that one."

Again, everyone laughed.

This is great, J.D. thought. After they got done with duties, they moved on to rules.

"Just a couple of basic ones," J.D. said. "Now, I know this is going to sound weird coming from me, but—no fighting."

He scanned the faces of the crowd. Aaron and Claire watched him most closely, but both of them nodded with the rest.

J.D. wondered where Bertram was. "Anyone seen Bertram?"

"He was taking a walk," Jenny said quickly.

J.D. nodded to Aaron. "You mind?"

"No, I'll find him." Aaron looked at Claire. She didn't look back. Their tension had already started to rise.

Another good sign.

When Aaron was gone, Claire's entire body seemed to relax. J.D. loved it when things worked out.

"No spitting," one of the girls called out.

Everyone laughed.

"Hey, I've got brothers," she said. "I've got a reason to say that."

J.D. nodded. "Yeah, no spitting." He exchanged smiles with Melissa. "Okay, serious note," J.D. said. "No hoarding of food. That's a big one. No stealing of food, no trying to muscle anybody to get more food."

Reggie hesitantly raised his hand again. "What's the punishment?"

J.D. had to think about that. "There are some spots up here we haven't mapped out too well. But they're big enough to get lost in. Someone breaks one of the major rules—exile, three days."

"Or they get to be invisible," Claire added.

"Invisible?" someone asked.

"No one talks to whoever broke the rules," Claire said. "No one lifts a finger to help them under any circumstances. Nobody makes eye contact with them. They're invisible."

J.D. liked that one. "Exile for three days or invisibility for a week. That'll be the choice. Good one, Holly."

"What's the penalty for lying?" Claire asked levelly.

"I don't know," J.D. said. "I guess we'll just have to wait and work it out."

"Guess so," she said.

The meeting broke up soon after that. Melissa walked with J.D.

"'Do the right thing. It will gratify some people and astonish the rest,'" Melissa said.

"Mark Twain, I love it," J.D. said. "And thanks—I don't think I could have pulled this off without you."

"Don't worry about it," Melissa said. "We're all in this together, right?"

He looked away, thinking about rewards. Bertram and Aaron, the dilo brothers...they each deserved a reward of some kind. Bertram had saved J.D.'s life. He had a lot of good ideas. If he was controlled just right, he could be a real asset.

Aaron, on the other hand...well, he had unfinished business with Aaron from the morning that they had both been zapped out of Wetherford. Aaron had humiliated him and had run when it was time to accept his punishment. He had led J.D. to the science lab and trashed the place. When the teachers came, he made sure they thought that J.D. had done all the damage. Had they gone back to the present, J.D. would have been thrown out of school. That would have destroyed his mother. Now there were rules and there were punishments.

Something could be arranged.

Light pressure tapped his backside, and he looked over. Melissa was using her tail. "Hey, where did you go?"

"Just thinking," J.D. said. "Good things. The future."

"Do you think there's any chance you'll tell me a little about the past?" Melissa asked. "You know, your past?"

It wasn't something that J.D. wanted to dwell on. Yet he saw the way people looked at him when Melissa was at his side. They accepted anything he had to say when he was with her, and she made things easier just by being there.

"Yeah, we can talk," he said.

"All right, when you're ready."

He nodded. When he was ready. That was cool. Very cool.

It was going back to being one heck of a good night.

CHAPTER 10

AARON

Aaron walked through the darkness surrounding the camp. He hated leaving Claire alone to deal with J.D. and his rules and stuff. And J.D. had been handling the fact that he knew who she really was completely wrong. But his words had really gotten to Aaron. Claire was acting as though she had a lot to prove, and maybe in *her* mind that was true.

Aaron couldn't help but think of stories that his dad and his dad's army buddies would tell late at night when they were sure Aaron was asleep. His dad had been in the armed forces all his life, and he had seen some pretty terrible things. Aaron joked around with his dad because the guy was such a pushover with him, and even called him Sergeant Charmin, but the truth of the matter was that his father was brave and wise—and he knew it.

The last thing you ever want in your unit is a soldier who's got something to prove, his dad had said to one of his friends. *They are dangerous to themselves and to everyone around them. I would rather have someone who is going to be able to make a calm decision based on the odds, not based on whatever problems they are carrying with them from back in the world.*

And now that Aaron knew that Claire was Claire and not Holly Cronk, that bit of wisdom from his father made him think. Claire felt she had a lot to prove, and that could make her dangerous.

Aaron kept walking. Ahead, he saw a flickering light. He felt the slight breeze and wondered if he was looking at a torch in the distance.

Following the light, he saw that it was bouncing off a high wall from a gap in the ceiling of a lower cave. He entered the cave, feeling around its contours. He walked quickly and quietly until amber light filled the twisting way ahead. Then he turned and saw Bertram in a small chamber, several dozen chunks of the M.I.N.D. Machine strewn around him on the litter that had been used to carry it.

Aaron was too shocked to say anything. This was incredible. Bertram had fashioned some rough tools and made a metal pot out of one of the machine's side panels. It rested on a pyre, and he was using it to melt other chunks of unneeded metal to slag. He was soldering and connecting things, and his eyes were glazed, as if he were only barely aware of what he was doing. It was like Bertram's hands and his body weren't under his own control.

"Bertram," Aaron said. "Hey!"

Bertram jumped, the glazed look vanishing. He stared at what was in his hands, and even *he* seemed surprised. Then he looked over at Aaron.

"You can't tell them," Bertram said. "No one can know about the machine."

"Why not?" Aaron asked. "Is there a chance? Can you make it work again?"

"I don't know," Bertram said. "I'm trying and I'll keep trying."

"We can mine for some gold. I know there's supposed to be gold deposits dating back to this era," Aaron said. "That might help."

"Okay, but you can't tell anyone. Not even Holly. Especially not J.D."

Aaron felt flustered. "You don't know what it's like out there. You haven't seen how everyone's feeling. They need something to hold on to. They need some hope."

"But not false hope," Bertram said. "The chances of any of this working are probably a billion to one worse than they were when I made the M.I.N.D. Machine by accident in the first place. It's one thing if I can go to them and say look, here, it's working. And it's one thing if I fail and I end up disappointed. But it's another thing if they know and then nothing happens.

"It's just better this way. Please, Aaron. I've made

mistakes. Please help me not to make another one."

Aaron stared at his fellow Dilophosaur. The bodies they were in were brothers, and he'd sensed that the dilo pack that attacked the group were more relatives. But he felt no connection to those crazed predators, not the way he did to Bertram.

Like Bertram, he was an only child. He didn't know what having a brother was like. Yet this felt the way he thought it should.

"All right," Aaron said.

"Marv and the others know," Bertram said.

"And you think they won't tell?"

"I know they won't tell."

Aaron stared at the remnants of the M.I.N.D. Machine, then looked away. "Can I get your advice on something?"

"Of course."

"It's Holly," Aaron said. "I'm worried about her."

Aaron told as much of the story as he could, expressing his concern without revealing Claire's secret.

"What would you do?" Aaron asked.

"People have to make their own mistakes," Bertram said. "It's the only way they learn."

"It's that simple, huh?"

"You care for someone, you watch out for them," Bertram said. "But nobody wants to feel like they have a baby-sitter."

The words resonated for Aaron. He'd had baby-sitters all his life.

"Thanks," Aaron said, holding out his hand.

Bertram took it.

For the first time in Aaron's life, he felt as if he really did have a brother.

CHAPTER 11

CLAIRE

Claire woke up in a lousy mood. She had dreamed that she was back in the present but still in her hulking scissor-jaw body. Even worse, she no longer had the power to communicate with her thoughts. Human beings ran from her or attacked as they would any monster, finally wounding her, chaining her, and dragging her through the street for crowds to throw rocks at.

It hadn't been a good time.

She lay on her side, her neck stiff. Above, the sky was still almost black, and the volcano was still spitting fire, but there were a few soft blue-and-gold streaks penetrating the ash-covered sky, letting her know it was morning.

She rolled to the other side, cracking the bones in her neck as she went, and stretched. A huge yawn was about to escape her lips when she heard voices from behind a ten-foot-high rock. As quietly as she could, she rose and peered over the rock.

J.D. was talking with Bertram in hushed tones.

"No, no, you can't do exact equal rations," Bertram was saying.

"Why not?" J.D. asked.

"We're not all the same size," Bertram explained. "You have to factor in the size and weight of each student depending on their dinosaur body. The amount of food needed to keep a Hypsilophodon going will be a lot less than what it will take to keep you going."

"I dunno," J.D. said. "We could be dealing with lunchroom mentality, y'know? In the lunchroom, everyone gets pretty much the same."

"In the lunchroom, some kids aren't two feet tall while others are twenty."

"Yeah, I see your point." J.D. laughed. "This is great, Bertram. I'm glad you signed on as my idea guy."

"Just want to do my part," Bertram said.

Claire got up, her body even more tense than before. Now J.D. had Bertram as part of his "team." Wonderful.

She heard footsteps and turned to see Aaron approach. She tensed. He'd been acting so strangely around her, making her feel that she was sending off the worst possible signals.

"Hey," Aaron said. His tone was so relaxed that it made her picture the way he was in the present, with his long hair and slacker clothes, hands in his pockets, a goofy smile on his handsome face.

The image made her relax. She nodded toward the border of the camp, and he followed her there. Then they took a walk through No Man's Land, the outlying plain.

"I'm not buying any of this 'kinder, gentler' J.D. garbage," Claire said. "Are you?"

Aaron shook his head. "Not really."

"And the whole thing that happened with Bertram and the machine when we were gone," Claire added. "The story holds up, but the timing is way too convenient."

She waited. Aaron said nothing. He looked up at her, listening intently.

"I'm gonna take him down," Claire said.

"J.D.?"

"He shouldn't be in charge."

"Everybody trusts him," Aaron said levelly. "They're happy with the way he's running things. What you're talking about wouldn't be easy."

"I know," Claire said. She appreciated that Aaron was keeping an open mind. "I can't exactly challenge him to single combat."

"I'd pay to see that," Aaron said.

Claire laughed. *This* was the Aaron she liked so much.

"I don't have a plan," Claire said. "Not yet. I just

need to know that I can count on you when the time comes."

"You know it," Aaron promised. "Just tell me what you need when you need it. I'll be there."

Claire smiled inwardly. "Great. What do you think about Bertram? Can we get him on our side?"

Indecision played across Aaron's features. "Maybe. But right now he's feeling pretty miserable, blaming himself for what happened."

"I don't think it was his fault," Claire said.

"I don't know," Aaron said. "From what I've seen of Bertram, the impression I get is that you'd have to come to him with proof. Solid evidence that J.D. did something wrong."

It seemed that Claire had some detective work ahead of her.

"You know this is risky," Claire said. "If we try to take J.D. down and it doesn't work—"

Aaron shrugged. "I'm in no matter what. I don't know what else I can say."

Claire wanted to kiss him but knew that would have been a very un-Holly-like thing to do.

"So, let's get started," Claire said.

CHAPTER 12

J.D.

J.D. walked through the camp, calling everyone by name and checking on their labors. Everything was going smoothly. Even Megan was calm and focused.

He had to keep himself from strutting.

The first day of the rest of his life had come, and J.D was feeling good. So good, he thought he'd step up the timetable on his revenge plan against Aaron. He thought about the line on the T-shirt Aaron had been wearing in the present: *Why put off until tomorrow what you can put off forever?*

J.D. wasn't the kind of guy to put anything off if he didn't have to.

The best part was that opportunity had presented itself in a surprising form: Reggie had asked—no, *insisted*—on taking at least one shift of menial labor each day. Today it was rations.

Well. Wasn't *that* interesting? Especially considering the crime Aaron was scheduled to commit.

"Hey," J.D. said as he approached the pachy.

Reggie had been on his hands and knees, counting out chunks of fish for the day. He had a cooking fire going. The moment he heard J.D., he snapped to his feet and turned to greet the great brontosaurus.

"Hey," he said simply. "Things are going okay. I'm just about set for lunch."

"Good goin', Reg," J.D. said. "I know everyone'll appreciate that. I sure do."

Reggie blinked several times.

"You got somethin' in your eye?" J.D. asked.

"No one calls me Reg," Reggie said. "I mean—I wish they would. Reggie sounds like a little kid's name."

"Yeah, well, you haven't been actin' like no kid," J.D. said. He nodded at the food stocks. "Doin' this when you don't have to, that's actin' like a man."

Reggie's shoulders fell back, and his chin went up proudly.

"I just wish that slacker Aaron understood how important this stuff is," J.D. said. "You know, the way you do."

"What'd he do?" Reggie asked.

J.D. hesitated. He didn't want to seem too eager to talk about this. "I should just try to work it out with him."

"No, really," Reggie said. "What happened?"

J.D. let a long, tired sigh escape from his lips. He

strained his long neck around to make sure no one else was close enough to hear them.

"I asked Aaron to take perimeter, but he didn't want to. He said he had better things to do."

Reggie's jaw dropped in surprise. The effect was comedic, and J.D. had to really restrain himself from laughing.

"No way!" Reggie said.

"I don't know what to do," J.D. said. "We didn't make any rules or set up any consequences for people who don't pull their weight."

Reggie looked down at the rations. "No. But there are other things we did set up..."

It took only a few more minutes for everything to be set in place, with Reggie thinking that J.D.'s plan was really his own. J.D. trotted off happily, wondering at how easy it was to play these people. If they had gotten back to the present, he would have gone there armed with a whole new way of looking at things and dealing with problems.

Laughter sounded, along with a piercing shriek. J.D. saw a group of dinosaurs gathered near the edge of the clearing, near the spitting lava. One of them, a Syntarsus, held some kind of homemade rag doll over the edge. It looked kind of like a teddy bear made of leaves sewn together with vines. It was floppy like a beanbag, so J.D. figured it was filled with earth or sand. Dawn, one of the smaller dinos,

was leaping up and down, trying to get at the doll.

"Oh, come on," the Syntarsus was saying. "You don't really care about this thing, do you?"

His buddies were all laughing. It was a low, crude, vile, and all-too-familiar sound. He'd heard it when he'd crush some dweeb like Manley into a locker for no apparent reason, or when he'd turn some other unfortunate loser into an object lesson back home.

Everyone thought J.D. liked the attention and even enjoyed going after those guys. The truth of the matter was that J.D. wanted to make it clear, in no uncertain terms, that he was to be left alone. He wanted everyone to know that he was strong, not weak, and that given the choice of being loved or feared, he'd take the latter.

That sound, that hyena laughter...He'd always hated it. That sound made him feel bad about himself and almost made him feel sorry for the losers he made examples of.

"If it falls, you fall," J.D. said simply.

The Syntarsus froze, along with all his buddies. His grip on the leafy teddy bear tightened, and a little *pfsss* sounded as one of the dinosaur's claws pierced the bear and made the sand inside it flow out. Two of the other guys started laughing.

"It looks like he just couldn't hold it," one said.

Then J.D. lurched their way—and stopped. The move had been enough to silence and terrify all the guys.

Dawn was still hopping up, trying to get her bear.

"Give it back," J.D. said. "Now."

The Syntarsus handed the bear back to Dawn.

"He's broken," she said. "I'll have to fix him."

"No," J.D. said. "*They* will."

The Syntarsus shook his head. "I don't know how to sew!"

J.D. took another step forward. The Syntarsus almost backed up—then he realized that he was already standing on the edge of the camp.

"Learn," J.D. said. "And no more of this. *Ever.*"

He turned, fully prepared to storm off—and

nearly ran straight into Melissa. He jumped. He couldn't help it. No one had even been able to sneak up on him like that.

"Well, now," Melissa said. "Look at you—protector of the innocent."

"Who'd have thought it, huh?" J.D. asked.

"Me." Melissa leaned in and kissed him.

J.D. was *stunned*. He watched Melissa trotting off, laughing. Then he thought of what he and Reggie had planned for Aaron.

He almost went back to tell Reggie to forget it. Almost.

But not quite.

CHAPTER 13

BERTRAM

Bertram was back in the cave, working on the machine. His job was to watch over the four little guys, which was perfect, because he knew better than anyone that they could look after themselves. He played with them during breaks but mostly let them do what they wanted. They were smart and capable, and he didn't worry in the least.

From outside, someone was calling his name.

Jenny!

He set down one of the control panels he'd repaired and turned, his foot getting caught in the vines leading from the litter. He tripped, and as he was sitting up, extracting his foot from the vine, he saw something strange. There were little nicks in the thick vine. Had Marv or Joey tried to chomp on the vines because they were still hungry after breakfast?

Bertram got to his feet and made it to the mouth of the cave, where Jenny and the others were waiting.

"Something's going on at camp!" Jenny said in a shrill voice.

"Someone's being judged!" Marv said.

Judged? Bertram thought. He frowned inwardly and accompanied the little guys back to camp. There he found the entire group in a circle. Aaron, J.D., Reggie, and Holly were arguing in the center of the circle.

Melissa stood nearby.

"What's going on?" Bertram asked.

"Aaron was hoarding food," Melissa said. "I found a whole supply he hid in a hole he dug over where he was sleeping."

Hoarding food? Bertram had not been present when the rules were being created, but they had been detailed for him later. He couldn't believe Aaron would do such a thing.

"This is wack!" Aaron shouted.

"First you didn't want to take perimeter duty, then this," J.D. said.

"I told you, I had something to do!" Aaron said.

J.D. nodded and gestured at the hole that had been uncovered. "Right. Like bury more food somewhere else?"

Holly surged forward. "He was with me. That's not a crime."

"And it's not against the rules to turn down a duty," Bertram said.

Everyone became silent and glared at Bertram.

"But it's not!" Bertram said.

Ugly-sounding murmurs rose from the crowd of students. Fred and Manley beat their spiked tails into the ground, and the dinosaurs near them raced away.

"No, he's right," J.D. said. "There's no punishment for refusing a duty, though maybe that's something we should think about."

"There's also no punishment for trying to subvert authority," Melissa said.

More voices rose up. Angry voices.

Holly roared and everyone quieted down. "J.D.'s not the authority. We all have an equal say in what happens to us." She looked down at the brontosaurus. "Or, at least, we'd better."

J.D. returned her level stare.

Bertram knew that he was far from the most liked person in camp, but someone had to keep this from going much further.

"Holly's right," Bertram said. "We need to be self-governing, not ruled by any one person."

Holly watched him cautiously. So did J.D.

"The thing is, no system's perfect," Bertram said. "Not in the beginning. Maybe not ever. The bottom line here is that all I'm seeing is circumstantial evidence. Aaron sleeps near that spot. Extra food was found there. Okay. But did anyone actually see Aaron take the food? Did anyone see him bury it there?"

Silence. All the students looked to one another.

Bertram felt relieved. This was going to be contained. It wasn't going to spiral out of hand as he had feared.

Reggie stepped forward. "I saw the whole thing."

Bertram recoiled. So did Aaron and Holly.

"He's lying!" Aaron said.

"It was the middle of the night," Reggie said. "I was having trouble sleeping. Then I started hearing these funny noises. Digging sounds."

"This is crazy!" Holly shouted. "Reggie's been kissing J.D.'s backside ever since J.D. saved his life. Can't you people see what's going on?"

"I saved Reggie's life," J.D. said quickly. "And Bertram saved mine. So what? None of that changes the facts." He looked to Bertram. "You have anything else to add?"

Bertram took another step forward. "This is one person's word against another's. There's no way we can know which of them is telling the truth."

"You got a point," J.D. said. "The problem is, we don't have a time machine anymore, so we can't all just go back and actually watch him do it."

The words stung Bertram into silence. Several of his fellow students hardened their stares at the reminder.

J.D. turned to Aaron. "Just confess and let's get this over with."

"I didn't do anything," Aaron said flatly.

J.D. turned to the crowd. "All right. One at a time. Everyone gets their say if he's guilty or innocent based on the *facts* presented here today. I say he's guilty."

"Guilty," Reggie added.

Fred and Manley yelled in unison, "Guilty!"

Aaron and Holly were among the last to voice an opinion. They both said, "Not guilty."

They were in the minority. Only the four little ones had joined them. Jenny looked to Bertram. His was the final vote.

"There's not enough evidence," Bertram said. "Not one way or the other."

"Twenty-three guilties, six not-guilties, and one wimp-out," J.D. said.

Several dinosaurs laughed at this.

J.D. looked to Aaron. "What punishment do you choose?"

Aaron stiffened.

"Exile?" J.D. asked. "Or invisibility?"

Bertram felt numb as he watched Aaron make his choice.

Things shouldn't be like this, he thought. *They can't be like this.*

Someone had to do something. He drew a sharp breath. *He* had to do something.

And he *would.*

CHAPTER 14

AARON

The moon was barely visible through a fine cloud of ash as Reggie the pachy, Sam the Syntarsus, and Bobby the Microvenator marched Aaron toward No Man's Land. Crimson streaked the night sky from the erupting volcanoes all around.

Reggie had head-butted him, and Bobby kept tripping and knocking into him. All three cackled.

Aaron had chosen exile over invisibility. J.D. had waited until night to send him away so that he could spend the day serving everyone their food while not being allowed a bite to eat himself. That hadn't been part of the prescribed punishment, just an added bonus J.D. cooked up that almost everyone went for in a big way.

One thing had surprised him: Bertram and Claire had spent a lot of time together. A part of him almost felt jealous, but then he figured it was natural. Neither of them was very popular with the rest of the "castaways" just about then.

An area of No Man's Land where there was a small water reservoir had been chosen for Aaron's little time-out, and Reggie carried three small fish that would be his food supply during his exile. Not much, but he wouldn't starve.

He was hungry now, and the smell of the fish was making him crazy. His every dinosaur instinct was to turn and attack Reggie for the food. But he kept himself together. He wasn't going to give J.D. the satisfaction of being able to extend his punishment for fighting.

Then he heard it. The chomping sounds. The smacking and crunching and burps.

Spinning, he saw Bobby eating the last of his food.

Aaron trembled with rage. "Bring more."

"I don't think so," Reggie said. "We're not going to be seeing any more of you for three days, remember?"

Bobby spoke up. "And if you break the rules and come back early, you'll get another three days!"

Sam only laughed.

Aaron turned his back. He knew they were just trying to goad him into doing something stupid. He'd scavenge and find something to eat.

Someone shoved him again. This time, Aaron tripped and banged his head on a rock when he went down. The smell of blood in the air, his blood, made his dinosaur senses flare. The rage he'd been bottling up threatened to explode as he leaped to his feet.

"No more," Aaron said. His claws itched. His body trembled.

Reggie lowered his big fat cueball head as if this were exactly what he had been waiting for.

"Come on," Reggie said. "Come get what you deserve."

Aaron thought about that. He considered the satisfaction it would give J.D. to know that he had fallen for yet another of the bronto's little traps.

So he turned and ran!

Angry voices rose behind him. But he had several advantages. He was a little faster than his pursuers, the wind was carrying their scents to him and not the other way around, and he had traveled this area with Claire previously. Behind him, the others stumbled or smacked into huge rocks. Aaron raced around, trying to decide if he would hide from the others until they finally gave up or if he would choose a spot and take a stand. A huge burst of lava from the nearby volcano lit up the plain for just a second.

Then, suddenly, a great shimmering darkness appeared before him. It was blacker than black, something greater than shadow, a complete absence of light and space and matter. He had seen black holes like this in the vision Will sent from the Dinoverse. He tried to veer away from it, but a force unlike anything he had ever felt before grabbed at him, adding to his forward momentum, dragging him in.

He looked back as he heard shouts and saw Reggie and the others staring at him in wonder. Then something pulled at him and hauled him into the darkness.

For an instant, he couldn't breathe. He felt as if he had been swallowed up into a void as complete and lifeless as outer space. Then there was a sudden wash of soft blue light before him, and not only could he breathe, but the air itself had dramatically changed. His keen saurian sense of smell detected the sudden loss of the humidity and fine bits of ash they had all been breathing. He smelled—

Air-conditioning.

The light he had seen was drifting in through windows. It looked like moonlight. Clear, perfect moonlight unhampered by clouds of black ash.

He stepped forward and felt as if he were tearing away fully from the darkness that had grasped at him. He heard soft, padded footsteps and looked down to see that he was standing on a red wrestling mat.

He was back in the present! Looking up, he saw that he was in the gym of Wetherford Junior High!

Aaron looked down and saw scales, claws, and brilliant flashes of color across his Dilophosaurus body. Was he dreaming? Had he fallen and hit his head again?

He turned around and saw a swirling black space behind him. The vortex was a door. He'd found a *door* between the past and the present! Only—he was still a dinosaur!

A switch was thrown and blinding light filled the gym. Aaron saw that he wasn't alone. Dozens of dinosaurs stood about him, circling him warily. Others sat on the bleachers, looking on with gnashing teeth and clicking claws as a trio of raptors approached.

"You shouldn't be here," the first raptor said. "And that *door* behind you can't be allowed to exist. Not if we're going to get what we want."

Who are they? Aaron wondered.

The raptors crouched, looking as if they were going to spring at any moment.

"Enough talk," the raptor said. He looked to his friends. "You guys know what needs to be done."

Aaron tried to prepare himself for the attack. There was no way out of this. He'd have to stand and fight.

No more excuses, Aaron thought. *Bummer, 'cause I was really hoping to use the one about dinosaurs eating my homework!*

Then the raptors leaped at him, claws and maws flashing.

The next thing he knew, it was raptor wrestling mania! Aaron grappled with the other dinosaurs, careful of their hooked front claws.

It took him only a few seconds to realize that the dinosaurs he faced *knew* how to fight. His dad had trained Aaron in several schools of martial arts, and in his travels, Aaron had picked up little tricks from street fighters and "devoted amateurs," true lovers of the fighting arts. He could sit down and watch a kung-fu film or some Hong Kong action film and know exactly what was real and what was being faked for the camera.

The guys he was fighting right now had been *trained*. The only possible advantage he could have over them lay in surprise. They would expect him to be surprised and disoriented and not to have any clue about real fighting, particularly in a dinosaur body. But he had been ready for a fight. Itching for one.

"You guys aren't from around here, are you?" Aaron asked.

The question surprised his opponents, exactly as Aaron hoped it would. He used their surprise to wriggle out of their midst. With a spinning kick he cracked the jaw of the first raptor. Dropping low, he sliced at the mat, then jumped back as he kicked stuffing from it into the face of another opponent, then hit the dinosaur with a simple roundhouse right.

The third raptor, flustered and not yet compensating for the fact that he was facing a real threat, came in with a kick to Aaron's left flank—just as Aaron expected. Aaron used his dinosaur speed to get out of the way, then brought his arm down on the out-stretched leg. He heard a sharp crack and a scream of surprise, then Aaron was racing for the exit.

The first raptor was getting to his feet. "The door you want is this way!"

Aaron heard the raptor's laughter.

"Where are you going to go?" the raptor asked. "Where can you possibly think you're going to go?"

Aaron had no idea. But it made sense to him that where one door existed, another might, as well.

He exited the gym with no other dinosaurs attempting to stop him. The corridor ahead was dimly lit. He glanced into classrooms as he ran, but every one looked deserted.

The dinosaurs he'd fought in the gym weren't Wetherford students. Aaron knew from the images Will had planted in all their heads that when the M.I.N.D. Machine had physically journeyed back in time, other matter had been displaced, and some students in the present had been given dinosaur bodies.

He had also seen some dinosaurs who didn't appear in the least bit confused or disoriented. They seemed to know exactly what was going on, and they intended to make the most of it for some dark pur-pose of their own. It had been a mystery, and now, for some reason, Aaron had been given the chance to solve that mystery.

He ran to the end of the hall, where he could

make a left and take the exit, or a right and follow another corridor. The exit doors were chained up, but through the windows in their upper halves he saw the blue glow from without filtered in, far stronger than moonlight.

Aaron wanted to check it out, but he heard footsteps from behind him and he ran again. He headed to the right, looking into the home ec room, shop, a history class with maps and globes.

He saw shattered glass, overturned desks, and other signs of a struggle everywhere.

What had happened to the humans and the transformed students of Wetherford Junior High? And who were the guys chasing him?

At the end of the corridor, to the left, lay the lunchroom. Aaron was starved. He could smell the delicious reserves of "mystery meat" and couldn't stop himself from bursting into the private entrance and tearing through the kitchen. He found meat, cold and leathery, and swallowed it up.

The running footsteps in the hall went past the door he had taken and dwindled. But there were other sounds that came from the cafeteria itself.

There was some kind of fracas. Aaron rushed in, worried that the students and faculty were there, being harmed in some way—

And got a face full of mashed potatoes for his efforts.

"Food fight!" someone yelled.

Aaron shook his head, clearing the food away, and got a good look at the oddball collection of dinosaurs who were scampering across the lunchroom, heaving containers of milk and trays filled with spaghetti or mashed potatoes or mushy brownie-like sludge at one another.

They were all meat-eaters, all tough-looking. With the exception of the raptors, they appeared strange in one way or another. Some might have been dilos like him, but their backs had more flexibility and their arms were twice as long. Others could have been Troodons, but they were almost human-looking—except for the scales and long, jagged teeth. Most of them hardly had tails.

And they were having an honest-to-goodness food fight! Aaron stole along the far wall, thinking of the vision Will had shown them of the Dinoverse. Its amazing architecture and its peaceful, evolved dinosaurs. The Dinoverse was a bright, hopeful reality where any dream could come true.

Aaron found a window and looked out, practically sensing what he would find before the nightmarish vision from his imagination became a reality.

Outside the window lay a city of tall, sterile buildings bathed in rich blue light, a city of wide walkways designed for intelligent, evolved dinosaurs, patrolled by saurians who carried swords and futuristic-looking weapons, a terrifying place that was every bit the equal and opposite of the Dinoverse.

He saw blue flames rise into the murky sky while black, insect-shaped flying machines buzzed across the airways. He saw huge, gentle plant-eaters being led around by predators. Glowing blue collars had been placed around the long-necks, and when one of them so much as looked in the direction of a fellow captive, the predator leading it used some sort of power baton. Rippling waves of energy pounded at the noble creature, forcing its head to drop and its knees to buckle.

Symbols glowed along the sides of buildings, and saurians looked up at them in alarm. Every living creature on the street hurried into some huge doorway and ducked out of sight. They used their batons to hurry the plant-eaters ahead of them as they cleared the streets.

Something was going to happen. Aaron could feel it.

Then he realized that the food fight in the cafeteria had stopped. The dinosaurs who had been battling now clustered around him, all riveted to the view outside.

"This is gonna be good," one of the evolved Troodons said with a snarl.

Lightning struck suddenly, but not from the sky. It appeared in the streets, raging against the buildings, blinding and terrifying. Aaron had to restrain a gasp as he saw negative images revealed by the lightning, glimpses of other worlds, other times, other realities.

He saw his own reality, but only for an instant— children playing by an open fire hydrant, couples holding hands and walking down the street. Then everyone froze as the lightning struck them.

He saw what had to be the Dinoverse, with dinosaurs of every kind blissfully walking about, their bodies becoming brilliant flares as the lightning struck them.

Other visions he couldn't even begin to understand played out before him. Worlds in which catlike creatures who walked on two legs chased each other across slick, glassy hunting grounds.

Primitive yet spectacularly beautiful places where creatures who might have evolved from plants ruled. Beings made of cloudlike matter flew across other twisted yet enticing landscapes. And butterflies the size of 747s settled in the streets of another.

In each case, the lightning struck, wiping out everything in its path.

Then, without warning, the lightning faded and the images disappeared.

"Outstanding!" one of the evolved Troodons said.

"I wonder how much longer before it's done?" another asked. "Can you imagine what it's going to feel like to be the only ones left?"

"I feel stronger already," a raptor said.

"The strong survive," the first Troodon said. "That's the law of nature. It's evolution."

"And the future's what *we* make it," the raptor said.

Aaron remained perfectly still. He felt when the group started to move away from the windows and fell in with them, doing everything he could to blend in.

He wasn't entirely certain of what was going on here, but he had an idea that if he could just get back to Bertram, *he* would know, and he would be able to figure out what to do.

To make *that* a reality, all he had to do was get back to the gym, to the doorway the raptors had been guarding.

Of course, if they were searching for him everywhere else, then it might not be that hard.

He went back to the hall, slipped down it, and hid in classrooms when he heard his pursuers. Soon, he was back in the gym, racing toward the black hole, the shimmering portal back to Bertram and Claire and all his friends.

It vanished just as he leaped toward it. Aaron landed in a roll, sprang to his feet, and heard applause.

The raptors were back. They had known he would return and had waited for him.

"You're not going anywhere," the raptor said. "So maybe we should pick up where we left off."

Aaron stood his ground as the trio of raptors circled him.

He had no idea what to do next.

CHAPTER 15

J.D.

J.D. was with Melissa, looking up at slices of moonlight sneaking between the clouds. He knew that he should have felt great. He'd gotten back at Aaron, at least a little, for what the slacker had pulled on him.

Yet he didn't feel great. He didn't even feel good.

Melissa nuzzled him. "Come on. I know today wasn't easy. But now people understand that the rules are going be enforced. They'll think twice before doing something that'll just hurt all of us, like what Aaron tried to pull."

That had been his "campaign platform," what he had told the others he honestly believed: *We have to look out for the greater good, for what's best for the group. We have to be strong.*

The strong survive.

In ways, it had just been a line. Oh, he meant it about being strong. But the rest...

"I'll be back," J.D. said. He broke from Melissa

roughly, making sure she knew that he wasn't playing around.

"Yeah, sure," she said. She sounded hurt, and he hated that.

J.D. walked past a dozen of the other students, who all greeted him with smiles and happy, trusting expressions. He kept up the "noble leader" facade as long as he could, then made his way toward the southern part of No Man's Land. Manley was watching the perimeter, or—well, he would have been if he weren't sound asleep.

J.D. let him lie there, worthless lump that he was, and walked into the darkness. He found an area behind a handful of two-story-high rocks. He had to wonder if Manley would hear if he just let himself go. The noise he'd made in the ditch yesterday had brought Aaron. It was a risk.

But he was so mixed up, so angry, and he needed to let it out, needed—

A blinding burst of blue-white lightning exploded all around him. He didn't even have time to shout in surprise before the reality of the Mesozoic crumbled around him, dropping away in shards like broken glass. He could see nothing around him, only an antiseptic whiteness.

Only—he could still smell the ash in the air. He could still feel the sodden earth beneath him.

At the same time, he could feel a smooth, cool

polished surface beneath him, like marble. And he could smell the cleanest, freshest air he'd ever smelled in his life.

J.D. thought of the vision Will had given them when he had reached out from the Dinoverse.

And he thought of who had been with Will.

"There isn't much time," a voice called.

J.D.'s body tensed at the sound of that voice. He knew instantly to whom it belonged. After all, he'd been listening to that voice all his life.

Turning slowly, he confronted the scientist Will had allied himself with in the Dinoverse.

It was *him*. A brontosaurus who looked just like him, except that the other dinosaur's eyes were weak and his entire body seemed weighed down by some imperceptible burden. J.D. was looking right into the eyes of the J.D. Harms who might have been.

Kind, intelligent, and compassionate.

Weak.

J.D. wondered if the others were seeing this, too.

"No," Jae'Dee Harms said. "What is done cannot be undone, yet kindness is welcome, especially in these unusual times. I have no wish to cause you further pain beyond what you have brought on yourself."

J.D. stared at the saurian. Beyond the brontosaurus, he saw some kind of lab and a crackling lattice of energy surrounding the other M.I.N.D. Machine.

"You know what I'm thinkin'?" J.D. asked.

"I cannot read your mind, but our thoughts are similar."

J.D. laughed. He didn't even try to restrain himself. "You're wired into my head. Fine. But don't try to kid a kidder. It's not gonna work."

He thought the most repulsive things he could possibly think about the other dinosaur. He released all the anger, all the rage that had been pent up within him, focusing it in a single psychic assault.

Jae'Dee Harms didn't even flinch.

What is going on here? J.D. wondered. Either this other version of him had been telling the truth about not being able to get into his thoughts, or he was tougher than he looked.

"There isn't much time," Jae'Dee said. "It isn't safe."

"Yeah, I saw what's happening in your world," J.D. said. "That doesn't have anything to do with me. I didn't ask for any of this. I'm just trying to make the best of it, that's all."

"You care about them."

"About who?"

"The other students. You don't want to admit it. Not even to yourself. You equate compassion with weakness. Caring with stupidity. And you despise your father for not doing what he could have done for your mother."

J.D. stumbled back. "Liar. I knew you were in my head."

Suddenly, another dinosaur came into focus behind Jae'Dee. It was a female brontosaurus, her face impassive, her features frozen. Yet there was a sadness in her eyes, one he had seen in his own mother's eyes so many times. It was the face of a woman in tears, though she could not cry.

"Jae'Dee, the machine is dangerous," she said. "This must be done. The warning has to be given. And he must be made to see."

She turned away and vanished into the pale white glow surrounding the other dinosaur.

"But you—you don't hate," J.D. said. "You can't."

"We can," Jae'Dee said. "Anyone can. It takes strength not to hate. It takes strength to forgive and to understand."

J.D. thought of his father, a doctor, who had turned down offers to move to Beverly Hills and make a fortune. There was nothing beyond what had already been done that could help to restore his mother's face, but his father could have alleviated the weight of his mother having to work to support them when his medical practice was failing. He could have made her happy. He could have given her anything she wanted.

"How do you know what she wanted?" Jae'Dee asked.

J.D. knew now that though the other dinosaur wasn't in his mind, he really did understand everything that was in J.D.'s thoughts.

"You consider your father selfish," Jae'Dee said.

"Yeah," J.D. said. Why not admit it?

"Did it ever occur to you that it may have been your mother who didn't want him to take the offers that were made to him? That she knew how moving would have changed him? What it would have done to the man she loved?"

J.D. stared at the strange, other version of himself. He felt as if he were being torn to shreds inside. "What does it matter? There's no goin' back."

"But there is going forward," Jae'Dee said. "And it will take strength."

"I can't do anything for you!" J.D. shouted. "The machine's gone. You *know* why."

"This isn't about us," Jae'Dee said. "This is about you and the other students. There is a river at the far end of your territory. If you cross it, you can escape the dawn of fire. You can save yourself. You can save all of them."

"What are you talking about?" J.D. asked. "What's going to happen?"

Suddenly, J.D. was surrounded by a vision of darkness and destruction. Fiery stones fell like cannonballs all around him. He heard screams, felt a sizzling heat, and knew there was nowhere on this plain that would be safe—not even in the high caves.

The volcano's eruption wasn't over. What they had witnessed was only its opening volley.

Their camp was going to be destroyed.

J.D. squeezed his eyes shut. "Make it stop!"

Suddenly, just it had begun, the "dawn of fire" stopped.

J.D. looked to his other self. "Why are you showing me this? Why should you care if we make it or not? What's in it for you?"

"We're both selfish," Jae'Dee said. "You decided the fate of everyone around you to satisfy your wishes. You're guilty of the crime you've been accusing your father of all these years.

"And I am, too. I can't save my world. But when the darkness comes, I want to know that I did what I could to save a world. Any world. Even yours."

Then J.D. saw a fierceness, a determination, a strength in the other J.D.'s eyes—and the devastating truth of his own weakness struck him full force. His body collapsed under him.

"It's not true, not true," he whispered as he shuddered with guilt and shame.

"Listen to me," Jae'Dee said urgently. "Listen and know this to be true: The world is what we think it is. If we can change our thoughts, we can change the world. It's really that simple."

Then the sounds around him changed. The slight crackling of the other dimension's M.I.N.D. Machine intensified. J.D. looked up quickly, just in time to see a rippling field of darkness appear before Jae'Dee. It reached toward him, but another figure was in its way.

"No!" both J.D.'s screamed.

In a heartbeat, J.D. watched the brontosaurus version of his mother get swallowed whole by the darkness. It touched the very edge of the M.I.N.D. Machine—

And the vision stopped.

J.D. was left alone in the darkness, shouting and screaming and struggling as if he were grappling with something that he could never defeat, no matter how hard he tried.

After a time, he became still. When he rose again, the same light that had been in Jae'Dee's eyes was in his.

He knew what he had to do. And he accepted that it wasn't going to be easy. But he couldn't let anything happen to the others. Not now. Not after what he had seen and felt. He had to honor the people who had put their trust in him. No matter what, he had to keep them safe.

He walked back to the camp, considering all he had seen and heard. Somehow, his counterpart had been through everything that he had. Yet Jae'Dee had summoned the strength to rise above the emotions that turned J.D. into what he hated most and made him unable to see his parents for who and what they were. He would never be able to tell his mother or father that he was sorry. But there were other things that he *could* do.

He would start by reversing his judgment on Aaron. Then everyone would be put to work moving the camp across the river. Once he had gotten everyone to safety, he would tell them the truth. He owed them that much.

"Hey, fungus-breath."

J.D. looked up. He saw a two-story-high dinosaur blocking his path.

"Claire," he whispered. "Listen—"

"No, you listen," Claire said. "There's something that you've just gotta hear. Come on."

She stomped back to the camp. She seemed triumphant. Happy.

Something twisted deep inside him. He followed her, almost afraid to know why she seemed so excited.

The entire group was gathered in the clearing just as they had been earlier for the circle of judgment.

"Wait," J.D. said. He sensed that something terrible was about to happen. "You don't understand. I've seen something."

"*You* don't understand," Claire said. "We don't *care*. Hey, Bertram, show him."

Bertram nodded stoically, and the four little guys hauled out the litter that had been used to carry the M.I.N.D. Machine.

J.D. felt sick. The evidence hadn't been

destroyed. He knew what was coming and that he couldn't stop it.

"What happened today made me think," Bertram said. "It made me question. Once I started asking questions, all the answers just fell into place."

"Don't," J.D. said. "You have to listen to me. We're all in danger. This area is not safe."

"Nice try," Claire said.

He saw the victory in her eyes and the hatred burning there. He knew how strong she felt and how false a feeling it really was.

"Should we get a sample of your bite?" Claire said. "Have you chomp down on some vines so we can compare and contrast? Or do you just want to confess?"

J.D. didn't know what to do. He had to have their trust. Their lives depended on it.

The lying had to stop.

"I did it," J.D. said, looking into Claire's eyes. "I sabotaged the vine because I didn't want to go back."

Dinosaurs rushed at him, pounded at him, screamed, bit, and clawed. J.D. didn't even try to defend himself. He knew he deserved all that was happening and more.

Claire and Bertram hauled his attackers away from him, but for every dinosaur they pulled off, two more took its place.

Then there was a huge explosion. J.D. saw Fred's

and Manley's spiked tails being yanked out of the earth beside him and rising above him, poised to strike again.

Claire jumped into their path. "No!"

The steggies hissed and roared.

"This isn't how it's gonna be," Claire said. "This isn't what we are."

Fred and Manley stared at J.D. with open hatred.

"Besides," Claire added, "which do you think would hurt him worse? Your tails—or what we discussed before we dragged him back here?"

Fred and Manley slunk away. J.D. couldn't tell if they had just been intimidated by Claire or if they were desperately seeking someone to lead them.

"Please, listen," J.D. said. He suddenly thought of the power that he had over Claire. Her secret.

"Holly, please."

Claire looked at him. There was another flash of fury in her eyes that was intermingled with fear.

He wouldn't betray her secret. He wasn't trying to use what he knew as leverage. But he didn't how he could ever convince her of that.

"I saw the Dinoverse," J.D. said. "That other version of me. He had another message. He—"

Claire rushed at him, maw gnashing. Her mouth went to his throat, and she roared.

J.D. stared into her eyes, trying desperately to think of a way to make her understand that he was sincere. Claire backed off and Bertram guided her away.

"You're such a liar," she said. "You'd say anything, wouldn't you? Make up any story. That one about Aaron was a good one, wasn't it? You have one about me? Do you think anyone would listen?"

J.D. understood what she was doing. Claire was safeguarding herself. She wanted to be certain that if J.D. told her secret, no one would believe him.

"Just listen to what I have to say," J.D. asked. "You've got to believe me!"

Bertram was shaking his head. "It doesn't make sense. Why would Jae'Dee reveal himself only to you? Why didn't we all see the vision? When Will reached out, he spoke to all of us. Why would Jae'Dee only talk to you?"

Because it was personal, J.D. thought. *Because he had to make me see the truth.*

But Bertram and the others were looking for proof. If only he could give it to them. How could he convince them that what he went through wasn't just a dream, a crazy vision that came from his guilt?

He knew that what he saw and felt had been real. How could he prove it to them?

"This place isn't safe," J.D. said. "The volcano's not finished yet. Jae'Dee said something about the dawn of fire. I don't know if it's when it becomes light again or when, but..."

"Enough," Claire said firmly. "He admitted that he

did it." She turned to J.D. "You set up Aaron!"

"Yes," J.D. said. "Don't blame Reggie. It wasn't his fault."

"Sure, he was playing the angles, like always." Claire turned to the others. "Guilty or innocent? The vote is all that matters now."

"Guilty," Fred said.

Manley echoed Fred's verdict.

One by one, every student in the camp said the same word, including Bertram.

Claire was the last.

"Oh, very, *very* guilty," she said. She sounded almost gleeful.

She stomped over to J.D. "But you don't get to pick your punishment. We've already figured that out."

She turned her back on him. Everyone turned their backs on him.

"Wait," J.D. said. "Listen to me. I know I made mistakes. Worse than mistakes. I know you can't ever forgive me. But please, you've got to listen. All I need is for you to listen."

They weren't listening. They went back to their tasks. He went to Melissa, and she seemed to not even know he was there. He stopped before Bertram.

"Please," J.D. said. "They'll listen to you. Please."

Bertram walked away. Only then did J.D. understand his punishment.

He had become invisible.

CHAPTER 16

BERTRAM

The next day, Bertram buried himself in work. He didn't want to think about what he had witnessed the day before. The judgment against Aaron, which he had tried to avert, and the judgment against J.D., in which he had participated.

By the time night had fallen, no one had been able to find Aaron. Almost every work detail had been brought to a halt for the search, but so far, it had been wasted effort.

Bertram was less concerned about Aaron than he was about Holly. He understood that while Aaron had a tendency to act like a layabout, he could be crafty and resourceful when necessary. He had been told to get lost for three days. Apparently, that was exactly what he'd done.

Plus, there was a feeling Bertram had, something that told him Aaron was not what should be concerning him just then. He listened to that instinct.

When the search parties had come anywhere near

Bertram's hidden "lab," one of the little guys had managed to steer them away. He hated having to keep his work secret, but he was determined not to raise anyone's hopes until—and *if*—he had reason.

Reggie led the searchers to where he and the others had last seen Aaron.

"We gave him his fish and he took off," Reggie had said. He didn't meet anyone's gaze when he spoke.

The group had agreed that Aaron could decide whether Reggie would be punished and what form that punishment would take. In the meantime, Reggie and the other two who had taken Aaron to No Man's Land kept quietly to themselves. The only thing that had been remotely surprising to Bertram was that Reggie's pals had stayed with him even though they hadn't been involved in the conspiracy against Aaron.

The worst of it had been J.D. The brontosaurus had been wandering through the camp and even tried to aid in the search. Bertram didn't like pretending that he couldn't see or hear J.D.

He was angry, there was no denying it, but seeing J.D. undergo this punishment was hard on him. He remembered all too well how it felt to be invisible, because he had been invisible, too. Before he had created the M.I.N.D. Machine, no one had really known that he was alive. Not in a good way, anyhow.

Focus, a voice inside him said. Mr. London's voice. His teacher, mentor, and friend.

"Yeah, Mr. L, I'm working on it," Bertram muttered.

A little voice spoke up. "Who's Mr. L?"

Bertram jumped. He hadn't heard Jenny enter the cave.

He looked down at the device he'd been fashioning. It looked different than it had the last time he'd really looked at it. Only—Bertram didn't quite remember what he had done to it. Every time he worked on the machine, he kind of zoned out.

"Mr. London," Bertram said. "He was my science teacher."

"I'm supposed to have him next year!" Jenny said. "He wears funny ties, and he's really nice."

"Right," Bertram said. "We were together when everything went haywire and I ended up back here with the machine."

"But he didn't come back," Jenny said. "Where did Mr. London go?"

Bertram frowned. He had no idea. In fact, he hadn't really even considered what had happened to Mr. London until that very moment. It was almost as if the part of his brain that had been capable of forming that thought had been turned off, as if—

Focus!

A shiver ran thought Bertram. He'd heard Mr.

London's voice again, crisp, clear, and demanding.

The voice had come from inside his head.

"I'm sure he's fine," Bertram said. "I'd better get back to work."

Jenny ran off to play. Bertram went back to work. This time, he didn't allow himself to fuzz over. He concentrated as hard as he could while his hands put pieces together as if they had a mind of their own.

Or one that belonged to someone else entirely...

"Gosh, golly, Mr. L, what should I do now?" Bertram asked.

The voice came again. There was a trace of amusement in it.

Go fly a kite.

Bertram actually laughed out loud.

The next two days passed in a blur for Bertram. He worked morning, noon, and night. The little guys helped him in every way they could, including in the construction of a large kite. The lightweight frame had been made from metal that had been salvaged from the machine but wasn't needed in the construction of the Mark II version. Stripped wiring had been painstakingly wrapped together to create a fifty-foot-long string that was fortified by vine.

After that, the whole crew waited patiently for rain.

By the fifth day, Bertram was getting seriously worried about Aaron. Reggie and the others had become more withdrawn than ever, and J.D. was still passionately attempting to get someone to listen to him.

"Hit me!" J.D. yelled at Fred. "Just do something. I know you can hear me. The fire's coming. The volcano's going to get a second wind. Please!"

Bertram watched J.D. plead with Melissa, only to be ignored, as usual.

The duration of J.D.'s invisibility hadn't been determined. It might last forever.

That night, Bertram had been out walking, collecting his thoughts. He had seen J.D. off by himself, lying on his side, staring with wide, horror-struck eyes at the volcano.

Then J.D.'s gaze had gone to Bertram. J.D.'s lips quivered. He almost spoke, but Bertram held up one hand.

"Don't," Bertram said. "We've all heard what you had to say. Just sleep."

J.D. nodded, waves of gratitude pouring from him. He settled back, his exhaustion finally catching up with him.

Bertram stood over the brontosaurus for a few minutes, then left when he heard others approach.

Six days after Aaron's disappearance, Reggie broke down and told the entire story of what had happened. He described the rippling black void and the way it had greedily swallowed Aaron up. He told how he and the others had run from it at first, then watched it for a very long time from behind a rock until finally it shimmered and dissolved completely.

Holly took the news hard. But for Bertram, the revelation had been galvanizing.

Then the storm he had been waiting for finally came. As the rains turned the lava to steam, Bertram and the little guys launched the kite.

Its wire slid through the small aperture in the ceiling of Bertram's "workshop" and led directly to the scaled-down machine that sat on a rock down below.

Bertram had hoped that the sight of the kite would not draw too much attention, and that no one would seek shelter from the rain in his cave. The little guys stood out front, ready to redirect any curiosity seekers.

"Okay," Bertram announced.

He looked at the small contraption before him. A keyboard, monitor, two large metal slats, and dozens of control panels sitting in a metal control unit. It was unimpressive to all outward appearances, a homemade PC, nothing more.

Bertram stared at the ceiling. "Okay," he said again.

Thunder roared. Lightning crackled.

An hour later, as the storm was dying down, Bertram sat in the corner, feeling like an idiot.

"Oh, yeah," Bertram said. "My science teacher is living in my head. Man, have I lost it."

He thought of Aaron, his *brother,* who was lost somewhere in the void. Then he got angry. Aaron shouldn't have been taken. He should have been here, where Bertram needed him. There was no one he could really talk to, no one who could truly understand what he was going through, except Aaron.

He started beating at the keyboard, typing in nonsense phrases, shouting and spitting at the contraption, almost as if he could force it to work by sheer will alone.

Suddenly, a bolt of lightning caught the kite. Crackling energy rippled down from above along the line and poured into the machine. The monitor flickered to life. The base unit ground and hissed.

Bertram leaped at the keyboard, typing in a sequence of characters that was completely alien to him. His fingers tingled, and he felt the current moving through him despite his efforts to ground himself and the machine.

A bolt of crackling blue energy whipped out from the computer, blasting at Bertram and sending him crashing against the far wall. Then the lightning died and the cave was silent and pitch black.

But it hadn't been dark a moment earlier.

He'd lit three torches while he was waiting. Bertram realized he could no longer feel the guiding presence that he had been certain was Mr. London.

He stared into the darkness and saw it shimmering. At its heart, he saw a pinprick of light that expanded until it assumed the form of a dinosaur that was just about his height.

Aaron stumbled through the doorway, which disappeared an instant later. He collapsed before Bertram.

"Oh, man," Aaron said, hugging the ground. "There's *no place* like home."

CHAPTER 17

AARON

Aaron stood before the group and told his story. He described the world he had seen out the windows of Wetherford Junior High and what little he and Bertram had been able to conclude about the plans of the dinosaurs he had fought.

Then Bertram told everyone about the machine.

As questions flew and excitement rose, Aaron watched J.D. The brontosaurus circled the group, anxiously keeping an eye on the volcano, which seemed to be dying down.

"So—how'd you get out?" Claire asked. "I mean, I know another door opened and you went through it, but you were there for five days. What happened?"

Bertram intervened. "Five days our time could easily have translated to five seconds of his time. There's no reason to think that time moved concurrently—"

"Actually, it did," Aaron said. "She's right. I was a prisoner for five days."

Bertram was surprised. "All right. So how did you get out? Did the door just open where they were holding you?"

"What about everyone else?" Melissa asked. "What did they do with everyone at the school?"

"I never saw them," Aaron said. "But I heard those guys talking about them. The students who ended up in the bodies of dinosaurs in the present were taken outside and kept in the blacktop area outside the gym. That part hadn't been changed. The rest were in the auditorium. Everyone was being fed, everyone was being looked out for.

"They kept me in the old music room with four guards. For some reason, it was important to them that no one be hurt and that all the groups stay separated. At least for now."

Bertram paced back and forth. He looked like he was examining all possibilities.

"What really had them wiggin' was me," Aaron said. "I know they didn't want me to hear what they were planning, but I just kinda lay back after a while, and they started talking like I wasn't there."

"That was part of your plan," Bertram said.

Aaron shook his head. "Naw. I was just bummed."

Everyone laughed, and it was a really wonderful sound.

"Yeah, it was part of my plan," Aaron admitted. "What they said was that something would be happening soon and it would change everything."

Bertram stopped. "And the door opening and you coming through wasn't part of the plan."

"No way," Aaron said. "They were buggin' big-time. So what do you think's really going on?"

Bertram studied the faces of the crowd. Aaron had the idea that Bertram was trying to decide if the other students would be able to handle what he had to say.

"Mr. London used to bring all these old science fiction books in for me to read," Bertram began. "He told me there were worlds within worlds, realities that were similar to ours but different. Or, at least, that was the idea in these stories. What if things had gone just a little differently?

"In the Dinoverse, the comet that was supposed to hit the earth lost a lot of its steam and took a small chunk out of the moon instead. Dinosaurs lived on, gained intelligence, and physically evolved.

"In the world Aaron saw, something similar took place," Bertram went on. "But in their world, things took a turn for the worse. Instead of losing their basic aggressive tendencies and focusing on philosophy and the betterment of their condition, these dinosaurs became focused on fighting among themselves. All that mattered to them was strength and weakness. The strong thrived, the weak were subjugated."

Everyone listened attentively.

"Then a day came when there were no new fields to conquer," Bertram continued. "So they went looking. Their science revealed to them that there were other realities. Weaker realities, as far as they were concerned. As far as they were concerned, only the strong survive. So they created the doors to swallow up those other realities a piece at a time, and a void in which all those pieces would be held, to be studied and later to be destroyed.

"That's my theory," Bertram said. "Only—something went wrong. When Mr. London turned on the M.I.N.D. Machine and he and I went through together, some basic law of reality went out the window. Wetherford became a nexus, a bridge from one reality to another. That's how the raptors Aaron fought reached Wetherford, and how Will was able to get from Wetherford to the Dinoverse.

"That nexus, that house of doors, presents some threat to what the dinosaurs who were trying to wipe out all the other realities had planned. So they had to control it, which they've done. At least until they've finished their work.

"I get the idea that whatever it is that's coming will *be* the end of their work," Bertram said. "It'll be the end of everything except them. And for some reason, they're scared of us. They're scared that we can do something to mess it all up for them. The question is—what?"

A quiet descended on the camp.

The rumbling from the volcano and the bubbling of the flowing lava filled the air, along with the buzzing of bugs and the whisper of a breeze that caressed each of the students in turn.

J.D. stopped circling. He stood and looked at Bertram.

"The world is what we think it is," J.D. said. "If we can change our thoughts, we can change the world. It's really that simple."

Aaron watched as Bertram pretended not to hear J.D.

"That's what the other version of me, the good one, told me the night Aaron disappeared," J.D. said. He repeated the saying twice more.

Bertram looked up. "No."

Claire rose and stormed his way. "Bertram, remember the punishment."

"No," Bertram said again. He locked gazes with J.D. "Jae'Dee appearing to you happened the same time as—"

Claire cut between Bertram and J.D. and roared. "The punishment stands!"

Bertram walked around her. "J.D. was telling the truth about the visitation. He lied about so many other things, but he was telling the truth about this. Jae'Dee's M.I.N.D. Machine opened the door for Aaron."

Aaron watched as Claire roared again in fury and frustration.

"We can't trust him!" Claire yelled.

Aaron didn't know if Claire was talking about J.D. or Bertram. But he was worried that the moment he had dreaded had finally arrived.

"Holly, don't," Aaron said. "This isn't the time for a fight. We need to listen."

"No!" she roared.

Melissa looked up. "'There is one thing that gives radiance to everything. It is the promise that there is something around the corner.'"

"G.K. Chesterton," J.D. said quickly. His eyes were alive with hope for the first time since Aaron had returned.

Claire roared even louder, but her roar was practically swallowed up by a greater sound. Aaron turned to the volcano, certain that the deafening explosion he had heard had come from there.

But the cone looked the same.

The sound came again.

KKKKRRRR-ROOOOMMMMMM!

Beneath Aaron, the ground trembled. He looked to the high hills directly above their sanctuary and saw a fiery crimson glow.

"We're on another volcano," Aaron said.

But the rumbling and explosions swallowed up his words. He saw fiery stones explode into the air as the first rays of dawn's light penetrated the black clouds above.

The dawn of fire had come.

Screams sounded as the fiery rocks arced midway in their flight—and came down right in the midst of the group!

Chaos took hold. Dinosaurs ran in every direction as some were singed or even struck full on by the streaking cannonballs. Aaron shoved one of the little guys out of the way and took a glancing blow to his shoulder. Then he looked up and saw Claire frozen in place, staring in disbelief at the oncoming projectiles.

Aaron was too far from her, and too weak, to do anything but watch as one of the missiles struck her full force, sending her flying back.

"Claire!" Aaron shouted.

He watched her strike the ground with incredible force and heard something snap within her. Then J.D. was rushing past him, shoving a Maiasaura out of the way as another fiery chunk of stone rocketed down and burrowed a channel in the ground beside them.

Aaron went to Claire's side. He heard the hiss of another stone and felt its blast as it landed beside him, knocking him from his feet. Then the explosions stopped.

He knelt beside Claire, whose eyes were closed. Her entire left flank was singed and wounded.

Her eyes flickered open, and she winced in pain as she tried to rise.

"Don't," Aaron said.

Soon, the others were gathered around them, though most kept a careful watch on the now-crimson peak high above.

"He called her Claire," Manley said. "Claire. I heard it."

"'Crystal' Claire," Reggie said. "She's not Holly at all. I always thought it was weird that Holly would talk so much..."

"Claire DeLacey," someone else said.

The name echoed throughout the group.

Aaron saw Claire's gaze turn cold and hard as she looked at him. There was a flash of fury in her eyes, then it vanished as she sank back in despair.

"We have other things to worry about," Bertram said. "J.D. was right. This area isn't safe. We have to get out. We have to cross the river. It's our only chance."

Aaron thought about the river. The current had been too strong even to permit fishing for food. Crossing it would be dangerous. Maybe impossible.

But the volcano on which they were standing was already rumbling, and the volley of stone that had been launched was only the opening shot. Aaron could see that stones had torn through the walls of the caves in the distance. Before long, lava would flow right through the area they stood upon.

If the group had listened to J.D.'s warning five days ago, there might have been time to plan and prepare.

Now they were just going to have to go for it—

And only the strong would survive.

CHAPTER 18

CLAIRE

Claire hated the way everyone was looking at her. Even J.D. watched her with eyes filled with sympathy.

"I'm all right," she snarled.

But that was a lie. She had been hurt badly. Lying on her side, she watched, chest heaving, as J.D. tended to the other wounded.

She didn't want him anywhere near her. She didn't want *anyone* even to speak to her. Fear and shame coursed through her as she considered what her life would be like as "Crystal" Claire once more.

Thudding footfalls sounded beside her. She looked over to see Fred and Manley. The spike-tails gazed at her silently and curiously. Then Reggie arrived, just to make the whole thing perfect.

"Hey, give her some room," Reggie said. He stood over her. "Claire, hon, believe me, there's no reason to be scared. I'm here now, and—"

A sudden explosive force struck directly behind Reggie, sending him flying to the dirt. He hugged the ground, trembling and crying.

"No more, no more, no more!" he squealed.

Claire looked beyond Reggie's quaking form to see Fred and Manley extracting their tails from the earth.

Reggie finally looked up, turned, and saw the steggies waving their tails in the breeze.

"Take off," Manley said.

Reggie scrambled to his feet and ran, totally ignoring the barrage of laughter that followed him.

Claire laughed. She couldn't help herself.

Then Fred and Manley came closer.

"Was it all an act?" Fred asked. He sounded genuinely curious and looked as if he was trying to make up his mind about something.

"It started that way," Claire said. "Then things changed."

Manley shook his head. "I don't get it."

Claire looked around and saw that everyone else had gone back to packing up as much food and fresh water as they could. "I'm not sure it's something I can explain."

"But you *were* scared," Manley said.

Claire nodded. "Facing things is always scary. It gets a lot less scary as it goes on. And sometimes not facing things is the scariest part of all."

Fred nodded. "If we can help, let us know."

They walked off, leaving Claire confused yet hopeful. Then she saw J.D. coming.

She roared and struggled onto one knee. With a grunt, she fell onto her backside, cursing herself for the scream of pain that left her.

She remained quiet while J.D. told Aaron and Bertram how best to treat her wounds. He left without even meeting her accusing gaze.

Bertram went off, muttering something about securing the machine, and that left only Aaron.

The mouth.

"I didn't mean for anyone to find out," Aaron said. "I couldn't help it. You were just standing there, and when that rock hit you—"

"Shut up," Claire said. She didn't want to hear any of it.

Aaron hung his head. "We've got to get you moving. The next round from the volcano could come in five minutes or five seconds."

Claire rolled onto her unhurt side. Pain more intense any than she had ever known coursed through her, but she was expecting it this time and only grunted. Then she let out a low, rumbling roar.

"If you want to make yourself useful, get Fred and Manley," Claire said. "Then take off and find someone else to help out."

"So that's how it is between us?" Aaron asked.

"That's how it is."

"I care about you," Aaron said. "I thought I could handle never going home so long as I could be near you."

"What part of 'that's how it is' didn't you understand?" Claire asked.

Aaron went off to find Fred and Manley. They came quickly, and she told them what to do. Soon, she was on her feet, Fred on one side of her, Manley on the other. She leaned on them both and flinched as her wounded flank rubbed against Fred's. It hurt, but it was the only way she knew to keep herself from falling over.

The entire group left the clearing. The scaled-down M.I.N.D. Machine was attached to Bertram with a makeshift rig. The cable and the kite were carried by the little guys.

Overhead, thunder sounded, and everyone jumped.

"It's not the volcano," Bertram said reassuringly. "We're just in for a little rain, that's all. That can be a good thing. Cool us off."

Claire looked around and studied the faces of the dinosaurs in the convoy.

She saw Melissa's downcast face and understood how betrayed and angry she must feel. She gazed at Reggie, who stared ahead sourly, and decided that he felt misunderstood and unappreciated.

Then she saw Bertram and the way he held himself despite the weight of the machine. His back was straight, his eyes clear. He looked excited. She couldn't see Aaron, but J.D. was there, his head bobbing on his long neck, his eyes wide and soulful.

He looked every bit the penitent and was playing the part extraordinarily well. But she wasn't buying it. She had been weak when he got to her. Now she had learned how to be strong, and she would never let anyone make her go back to being what she had been.

Not J.D., not Aaron. No one.

Suddenly, Melissa was walking close to her.

"Claire," Melissa said. It sounded as if she was trying out the name to see if it fit.

"What is it, Melissa?" Claire asked.

"Back in Wetherford, did you even know who I was?" she asked.

The question surprised Claire. She couldn't think of anything to do except tell the truth.

"No," Claire said.

"You don't know what it's like, do you?" Melissa asked. "Being invisible, I mean. It's not so great."

What was she talking about? Claire wondered. Was she starting to fall for J.D.'s act again? Was this about how she had wanted J.D.'s punishment *never* to end?

Claire waited.

"You went from being one girl who was in the

spotlight to another," Melissa said. "Most of us have no idea what that kind of attention is like. I'm betting there's a big downside to it.

"I don't have a clue what it must be like to have everybody running to pick you up when you fall because they think you're weak. I can't imagine what it would feel like to have everyone running to get behind you because they think you're strong."

Fred looked over. "Hey, Melissa, come on. This isn't the time—"

"This is exactly the time," Melissa said. "There may not be any other time."

"What is it you want?" Claire asked.

"Just for you to play pretend one more time," Melissa said. "Pretend you're the kind of girl who gets up every morning and goes to school hoping someone like Claire DeLacey or even Holly Cronk will notice you and talk to you. Hoping someone like that will want to be your friend, so at least you're some-one."

Claire wasn't sure what to say. "Melissa, you *are* my friend—"

Melissa cut her off. "Stop pretending. When I saw Claire DeLacey in the halls, I'd think, look at her, she's so strong. Why do they call her 'Crystal' Claire? Why do they treat her like she's gonna break?"

Claire was stunned. "You thought I was strong?"

"I used to," Melissa said. "To go to Los Angeles

on those auditions. To stand up in front of everyone and risk being laughed at during the plays and to have everyone applaud instead.

"To put up with jerks like Reggie and be patient with them when you could have just lost it at any time. I would have."

"You have no idea," Claire said.

"That's where you're wrong," Melissa said. "I do have an idea. I have more than an idea. I'm not the one who needs to buy a clue. That's your role now."

Melissa strode off, sad and angry.

"Don't listen to her," Fred said.

"Yeah," Manley added. "If you want, next time we'll make sure she gets lost before she can start on you."

The steggies raised their tails and slammed them to the ground.

Claire looked down at their expectant faces. They were waiting for praise. Waiting to be told how much she appreciated the offer.

Don't do me any favors, guys, she thought. But she said nothing. She had been weakened by the hit she took, and she needed them.

She was back in the trap. Even in the body of a two-story-high predator, the meanest creature on the planet, probably, she was back to being "Crystal" Claire, and if these guys dropped her, she probably *would* break right about now.

"I'll let you know," Claire said.

Fred and Manley seemed pleased with that. Claire looked over to Melissa, who was walking alone, her chin high, and she envied the girl her strength.

All she wanted in the world at that moment was to feel that she could get around on her own again, that she could protect herself and that she could say the kind of things Holly would say.

But the strength had gone out of her. With her head bowed, she limped with the others to the river.

CHAPTER 19

J.D.

J.D. "Judgment Day" Harms felt as if judgment day had finally come for him. He approached the river with the others and heard another volley of fiery rock explode from the volcano above. Again, dinosaurs rushed for cover, and again, there were injuries.

Though he had learned a great deal about the healing arts from his father, J.D. had few of the raw materials he needed to help those who were hurt.

He could, with the help of others, fashion splints to hold broken limbs, wrap tender ribs, and reset dislocated joints. He patched up cuts and scrapes and tried everything he knew to take a student's mind off what was going on when stitches had to be done. Sam the Syntarsus and his buddies, who'd been forced to learn how to sew to fix the doll they'd damaged, were his surgeons.

He could teach the injured to use pressure points to redirect the pain. He could monitor his "patients" to make sure they didn't aggravate their injuries by scratching at wounds with their sharp claws or by overexertion.

But it wasn't enough. What he wanted was to make things better. To make everything right again.

That was impossible.

Ahead, Bertram and Aaron stood at the bank of the river. The clouds parted, and a dim golden light played over the crashing water.

"It's thirty yards from this side to the other," Bertram said. "I wonder how fast the current is running."

Aaron tossed a rock into the water. The stone struck the rushing tide and was smacked back into the air. It flew high and was shattered against a larger stone.

"Fast enough," Aaron said.

The river flowed down from a wide crevasse so high that J.D. couldn't even see its apex. He'd heard Bertram talking about how the elevation of these peaks was so great that they would collect rainwater right from the clouds. The water had gathered momentum as it rushed down for miles to hit this point.

The land around them was a crazy quilt of planes and peaks, of jagged rises, deep caves, and wide, yawning mouths where lava bubbled and spat. Over the years, the geography had changed constantly.

Claire came over with Fred and Manley's help. "How deep is it?"

Bertram shook his head. "I can't tell."

Groaning with effort, she picked up a boulder in her maw and tossed it into the water. Foam rose as it struck, making a deep indentation and causing violent ripples. It sank about a half-dozen feet.

"Not too deep," Claire said.

"For you," Bertram added, nodding toward the little guys and most of the dinosaurs gathered around.

"If we had someone else who was tall, like Claire, we could get them to the other side, then run a line between them," Aaron said. "The smaller dinos could go across the line hand over hand."

"We don't have anyone else her size, Einstein," Fred said. "Try again."

J.D. stepped forward. "What about a dam? Or something *like* a dam?"

Claire's head snapped in his direction. He waited for her to say something like *What we need is for you to keep your stupid mouth shut.*

But she was silent.

Bertram looked intrigued. "What do you mean?"

J.D. took a moment before answering. He wasn't pausing for dramatic effect or trying to calculate the angles. He just wasn't sure if his idea was more likely to save them all—or send the bunch of them crashing downstream to the ocean, battered and broken.

"I'll tell you," J.D. said. "But I can pretty much guarantee no one's gonna like it."

He told them what he had in mind.

J.D. stood back while the group debated.

KRA-THOOOOOMMMMMMM!

He was the first to see the volcano spitting rock once more, and he frantically raced toward the others to warn them.

This time, the eruption was small, and the injuries few.

"We have to try," Bertram said finally. "I don't see any other way."

Neither did anyone else.

Soon, Claire was alone, lying on her side, while Fred and Manley got to work. They brought down trees and rolled the trunks along with heavy boulders from the higher shelves of land into the riverbank. Others dug and tossed earth in around the trunks and the rock.

"Keep it comin'!" Aaron said. "We need it Ph.D. stylin'!"

"What's that?" Claire asked in a small voice that possessed none of the fire of Holly Cronk's.

"Ph.D.?" Aaron asked. "Piled high and deep!"

She laughed despite herself, and J.D. was glad to hear it. Then her craggy features wrinkled up in pain and her little arms went to her wounded side.

J.D. rushed forward without thinking.

"Keep away from me!" she yelled as she saw him approach.

J.D. froze, and he saw the stares he had drawn from the others. "Someone do something. Please. Her side."

Claire looked down, and her head bobbed as she saw the wound had torn open. Sam and a couple of other dinosaurs crowded around her. Reggie came over and started making his old macho noises of reassurance, and Claire suffered in silence.

A rustle came from behind J.D. He looked back to see Melissa shoving at a large rock with her front paws. They stood side by side, two sauropods the size of VWs, and with their combined strength, the rock rolled forward. They shoved it until it splashed into the water with the rest.

J.D. saw that the dam was taking form. The river did not descend the mountainside in a smooth decline. It looked that way at first, but a close examination showed that the land had been worn down into ledges or shelves.

By blocking one of those shelves with rocks and trees and earth, they were creating a corridor where the water arched *above* them, then continued on its way.

J.D. stared at what they were accomplishing.

"Outstanding," he said softly.

"It is better to be happy for a moment and be burned up with beauty than to live a long time and be bored all the while," Melissa said.

J.D. turned to her. "Who said that?"

Melissa angled her head to one side. "I think you did, just now, with that look."

J.D. wasn't quite sure what to make of that. He was just so happy that Melissa was talking to him at all.

"Let's get back to work," she said.

Together, they became part of the Heavy Movers team, rolling rocks into the river, then stepping onto the safe ledge to help buttress them.

Inside three hours, they were within ten feet of the shore. Then J.D. heard the rumbling above. At first he tensed, thinking that the pressure of the river was beginning to break apart the dam. Or that another explosion of molten rock was about to spew.

But only a soft rain began to fall. The golden light of day could still be seen, but fresh cool water came anyway.

"Summer shower," Melissa said. She looked up and laughed. "In stories, it's like a symbol. Rebirth. Renewal."

"Yeah," J.D. said. He let the tension drain out of his body.

Nearly all of the group was on the shelf now, helping to extend the dam to the other side. The river water rushing above their heads was fierce, but the tallest of the students kept their heads down, and Claire was still on the other shore.

Then, as another huge stone was rolled into place, J.D. heard thunder again and felt the rain thicken. Overhead, the river water became more urgent. It pulsed and pushed harder, like a frustrated opponent that no longer wished to be denied.

J.D. saw the danger first.

He was about to shout a warning when a crack formed in the face of the dam and a stone blasted right into his face. He grunted with pain and shock, then stumbled back toward the edge of the shelf, where the raging torrent of the river waited to carry him to the sea.

CHAPTER 20

CLAIRE

She watched it happen from the shore. J.D. shouted as the stone and the blast of water struck him, forcing him back. He teetered on the edge of the shelf for an instant, then shifted his weight and fell forward, easing himself out of harm's way. Melissa rushed to his side as the water burst forth from the breach.

Claire rose on one knee, balancing herself with her tail. She ignored the pain as she watched the others frantically rush toward the breach in the wall. Fred put his head down and plowed toward it, jamming his heavy bulk against the roaring tide. He struggled to hold himself in place, and other dinosaurs arrived to help him.

He winced in pain, roared, and growled but didn't yield. J.D. stood on his hind legs and pressed his hands against Fred's flank, ignoring the gash in his forehead.

Melissa stood with him.

Claire stared at J.D., her anger nearly consuming her.

He's doing it again, she thought. *Playing everyone.*

Claire looked to Manley, who was frantically bashing the last tree on their side of the river to toothpicks. One of the logs he had already amassed fell from his high perch, and Claire steeled herself as it rolled her way. It struck her wounded flank, but she did not cry out. Instead, she worked the log until she was able to get it under one arm, and rose, using it as a crutch.

She saw the rain worsening and the flow of the river gaining in strength. There wasn't enough time for the others to finish the dam. The sections they had already completed would break apart long before then, and everyone would be slapped down by the river, crushed by the current, the rocks, the falls.

There was only one way to save them, and she knew that no one would listen to "Crystal" Claire if *she* told them what it was. So she would let her actions speak for her.

Balancing herself on the crutch, Claire took her first painful step. She reached the shore, where the dam began, and stopped as Reggie raced before her.

"It's not safe, the water'll knock you over," Reggie said. "Just wait here, I'll get Bertram or someone, I'll—"

She brought her head down and cracked skulls with the pachy. He wobbled for a couple of steps, then dropped facedown onto the shore.

She moved onto the shelf.

The high flow of river water leaped over the dam and struck her head and shoulders, nearly spinning her around. She fought to maintain her balance, then ducked low enough to avoid the torrent.

Moving across the shelf with slow, shuffling footsteps, Claire avoided the questioning stares of her classmates and ignored their pleas for her to go back.

They didn't understand, but she would show them. She would prove once and for all that she wasn't "Crystal" Claire, that she wouldn't break, that she could do what needed to be done and wouldn't be afraid or weak.

Above, lightning arced across the sky. Thunderclaps brought gasps from the students working on the dam. Claire saw Fred, J.D., and Melissa still holding the breach. At the very end of the corridor, Aaron and Bertram were facing a wall of stone. The dam was off to their left, the wall directly before them. By moving this wall back while adding to the dam, they extended the corridor.

Bertram carried the machine in a harness and the little guys carried the kite and its line. Aaron was hauling rock and chucking it into place.

Claire looked down at them. She knew that she had to play this just right. Play *them* just right. It was the only way.

"I just want to be here," Claire said. "If there's another breach, I want to be here to help."

"Thanks," Bertram said.

Claire nodded and looked away quickly. That hadn't been so hard. Now she just had to find some way to get them away from the wall just ahead so that she could—

"She's lying," J.D. called.

Claire turned so quickly that she nearly fell off balance. She stared into J.D.'s eyes and saw that he knew.

He couldn't stop her. None of them could. But they could make this a whole lot harder than it had to be.

"She thinks the wall won't hold, that she has to break through right in front of us, then use herself to hold back the river," J.D. said.

"Claire," Bertram said, "you're wounded. You're not strong enough—"

She wasn't up for a debate. She surged forward, hoping Bertram, Aaron, and the little guys would show enough sense to get out of the way.

But Aaron darted in front of her, pressing his back against the wall.

"What are you doing?" Claire asked.

"Keeping you from making a mistake," Aaron answered.

"Move or I'll move you," Claire said. Her voice quavered, but only a little.

"No," Aaron said. "You want to do this, fine. But I come with you."

Claire shuddered. She tried to picture Aaron surviving what she had planned.

But then—her plan had been to save them all. If he couldn't survive, then none of them could.

Not even her.

She looked back to J.D., her body shaking. "This is your fault!"

"Maybe," J.D. said.

How did he know? she wondered. *How did he figure out exactly what I planned?*

"It's what I would have done," J.D. said. "If I had been in your place. We're the same."

"I'm *nothing* like you," Claire screamed. "You stinkin' liar!"

"Before, I was lying," J.D. said. "I was lying to everybody, I was lying to myself."

Claire stared at him, her chest heaving.

"I know why you hate me," J.D. said.

"Shut up," Claire snarled. "Shut up or I'll toss you right off this ledge. I will."

"I know," J.D. said. He sounded sad. "But if you do that, there's no going back. Is that what you want? Do you really hate being who you are that much? I know I did."

Claire couldn't believe what she was hearing. J.D. was saying that he had changed.

She'd never believe that. Never!

"He's right," Aaron said.

Claire whirled on him, spit and foam flying from her open maw. "Shut up!"

"You hate him because he's changed and you haven't."

She advanced on Aaron, her crutch nearly breaking beneath her.

"Get out of the way," Claire cried. "It'll work. I can *make* it work."

"You don't have anything to prove," Aaron said. "Not to me. Not to any of us."

"I *have* changed!" Claire screamed. "I'm strong now. And I can prove it, so get out of the way!"

Aaron shook his head. "I told you before. You go, I go."

She darted his way. He didn't move. Didn't flinch.

Her shoulders sagged. "Don't do this. Please."

Overhead, the flowing tide grew stronger. The roar of the water grew louder. So did the thunder. Finally, the golden glow from above faded to gray.

From somewhere down the corridor, leading back to the dangerous shore, a sound came. Another crack was forming in the dam.

"There's still a bunch of us on the bank," Aaron said.

"Just move!" Claire shouted desperately. "Let me do what I've got to do!"

"No," Aaron said.

J.D. looked at them. "She's right. We can't hold

the wall. But we can hold *part* of it."

Bertram ran toward the shore. "Everyone! You've gotta come over now! Hurry!"

Ten more dinosaurs flooded into the corridor, Manley at the very end. Right behind him, a hole burst in the dam.

He shrieked!

Claire turned and tried to run, but she knew she couldn't make it in time. She hobbled and almost fell, feeling weak and powerless as the water flooded in behind Manley and rock crumbled his way.

She could see what needed to be done. But would anyone listen to "Crystal" Claire?

"The dam, bring it down behind you!" Claire shouted. "Form another bookend like the one by Aaron. Do it! Hurry!"

Manley didn't hesitate. He looked back and smashed at the wall of the dam with his tail, bringing even more of it down. The rock fell and piled up.

"Shove it into place! Hurry!" Claire said as she got closer to him. She wanted to help, but the water was flooding into the corridor and rushing at the smaller dinosaurs.

"Hold on to me," she said. "Hold on!"

They did.

Manley kept piling stones until the water stopped flowing in. The corridor was now sealed at both ends.

Claire looked down at the river as it flowed below

the dam and then down to the shore. Lightning struck in the distance. Dinosaurs clinging to her shook. She realized that she was shaking, too.

Just like "Crystal" Claire, she thought. She was shaking just like that weak little—

She looked at J.D. and saw that *he* was shaking, too. The sight quieted the voice in her head. And the look he gave her made it vanish forever.

He'd been right, and she could hardly believe it.

She mouthed the words *thank you*.

He nodded, and together they held the wall.

CHAPTER 21

J.D.

The rest of the crossing took close to an hour.

They moved the wall before them closer to the safe shore while collapsing the wall behind them, until the way was finally clear to the other shore. They scrambled up to the opposite clearing just as the volcano spat more fiery rocks.

The stones didn't reach the river.

"We're safe," Bertram said. Everyone cheered.

Aaron approached J.D.

"Look," Aaron said quietly. "If we get back—"

"*When*," J.D. said. "When we get back."

Aaron nodded. "It's just—I've been thinking about what I did to you at Wetherford. And about what you've done here. It took a lot of guts, what you did, admitting when you were wrong, taking responsibility, that took a lot of guts. I just want you to know that when we get back, I'm gonna—"

Aaron's voice was cut off by a series of growls.

They came from behind a set of stones on a slight rise to their left.

"Oh, no," Aaron whispered.

J.D. smelled the predators before he saw them. The Dilophosaurus pack emerged from behind the stones, looking energetic, well fed, and up for a battle.

"Form a semicircle," Bertram yelled. "Keep the river to our backs."

He called for the Heavy Movers. Fred, Manley, Claire, and Aaron responded. Even Reggie lined up.

The rain was worse. The sky was black. There were no reddish hues from the lava to help them see. Soon there would be darkness and chaos.

J.D. knew that the dilos could be held at bay for a while, and some of them might even be put down. But in the end, they would win. The dilos had every advantage. They would wear the protectors down. Attack and retreat. Stab and slash and wait.

There was food in this area, or else the dilos wouldn't be in such good shape.

J.D. thought of all they had done, all *he* had done, to ensure their survival, to make things right again.

It hadn't been enough.

A roar sounded behind the dilos. J.D. looked up in surprise along with everyone else there. A burned, scarred scissor-jaw emerged from cover and began to attack the dilos from their rear flank.

"Hey," Aaron said. "Claire, that's the one that you fed, that's—"

"Yeah," she said.

She crouched and readied herself for the inevitable attack, and within seconds, two dilos were upon her. A third was grappling with Aaron.

The appearance of the other scissor-jaw, who was *helping* them, almost gave J.D. hope. But still, he sensed deep down that it was only a matter of time.

A matter of time.

J.D. turned to Bertram and gestured at the rebuilt M.I.N.D. Machine. "I think now would be a good time."

"You don't understand," Bertram said. "I have to find some way to ground the operator, to provide insulation. I've got so much to work out..."

J.D. thought about it. The kite went up. Lightning struck it. Electricity rippled down the line—right into the machine and whoever was operating it.

"But—you don't have the dexterity," Bertram said, as if he knew what J.D. was thinking. "You can't type in sequences, and you don't know what they are. I don't either. Not anymore!"

J.D. thought of his counterpart's words: *The world is what we think it is. If we can change our thoughts, we can change the world. It's really that simple.*

"Let me do it," J.D. said.

"But the lightning, the rain," Bertram said.

J.D. watched the battle raging around them. He nodded toward the combatants.

"There isn't much time," J.D. said.

Bertram surveyed the area, then called to the little guys. They had the kite in the sky and the machine on a flat rock in moments.

J.D. heard the roars of Aaron, Claire, Fred, and Manley as they fought the dilo pack. He tried to clear his mind, to focus on what was important.

His world. The existence he had wanted to leave behind.

The people he had wanted to leave behind.

The thoughts filled him with joy. The images in his head, from his childhood—a Christmas with family, an unexpected kind word, a loving gesture—all filled him with a serenity he had never been able to achieve before.

He thought of something he had read: *Peace, like every other rare and precious thing, isn't something that just comes to you; you have to seek it out.*

"I'm ready," he said.

Suddenly, lightning rippled overhead. Energy tore into the kite and raced down to the machine.

Ahead, a dilo broke through their defense and ran right for him. J.D. watched it, unafraid.

This is meant to happen, he thought a moment before the energy hit the machine.

Then he saw Melissa blindside the dilo, stamping it to the ground with her strong front paws. She looked his way and called his name.

The energy was within the machine, and tendrils of blue-white lightning reached out, encircling him. J.D. felt his heavy body trembling, tingling, and a terrible agony threatened to overwhelm him.

From the corner of his eye, he saw strings of symbols racing across the screen, as if a ghost in the machine were manipulating its keys. But the ghost needed more. J.D. knew that. It needed his will, his desire to make everything right again.

J.D. supplied it. He no longer cared what happened to him. His only thoughts were of the life he had left behind, the life he wanted to give back to all the others.

He dreamed a world that was not the Dinoverse, not remotely a paradise, but not the dark place Aaron had seen either. He dreamed of a place of light and shadows, a reality of despair countered by hope, of fiery anger put out by endless, flowing love.

He dreamed the future.

Suddenly, there was a burst of pure white light, and J.D. felt a vortex open before him. His mind, his essence, was lifted up and out of the heavy body that had held it, and he stood in a whirling tunnel in which he could see dozens of realities forming and unforming around him.

He saw now that it wasn't enough to make it right for his world. He would have to do more.

It was within him, he knew. The power, the strength, to remake reality, his reality, *every* reality, any way he saw fit.

But all he wanted was to make things the way they had been. To let others decide for themselves how they would live their lives.

He plunged deeper into the swirling whirlwind of energies, hoping someone would remember him kindly, and perhaps understand why he had done all that he had done—and forgive him.

Then the energies tore into him, pulling him apart, and he did not fight them. He saw all the realities Aaron had described and more, and the darkness reaching out from one of them, scarring and attempting to destroy the others.

He thought of light. Of the pure, undiluted light of love that he had seen in Melissa's eyes near the end.

Letting everything else go, he let that light fill the world.

All worlds.

Then he was gone.

CHAPTER 22

AARON

Aaron opened his eyes.

He wasn't sure what to expect. One second he was fighting a Dilophosaurus, using all the skills he possessed to take the crazed dinosaur down, the next—

There had been a light. A brilliant, comforting light. The rains had vanished. The angry predator reaching for his throat was gone.

Aaron heard voices in the light. Millions of voices.

Looking around, he saw fluorescent lighting, pale green walls, black marble science lab stations, and a bunch of broken glass. Groaning, he sat up and found himself staring into the distinctly human face of J.D. Harms.

They were back!

Several teachers stood nearby. They looked disoriented. Two were holding on to each other for support. Then they turned suddenly and each straightened his jacket.

"I did it," Aaron said. He watched J.D.'s dark eyes and studied the other student's intense, stony features. "I broke everything."

J.D. raised a hand. "I—"

"No," Aaron said. "It was me, the whole thing."

He got up and faced the teachers. "I did this to make J.D. look bad. I figured you'd believe me and not him. I wanted to get him off my back. I should have just...It wasn't the right way to deal with things."

He felt someone lightly tapping his shoulder.

Aaron looked back. J.D.'s eyebrows were raised. He appeared to be a little out of it.

"Hello," J.D. said.

Aaron turned from the bigger student. "Did everyone hear me? It was *me*."

The closest teacher threw up his hands. "Both of you, after school. If there is an after school."

"The insurance companies are gonna fry us," another said.

The third teacher wandered off, his hand to his head. Without looking back, he said, "You boys stay here and try not to move around too much. We'll have ambulances and stuff. Yeah, ambulances. Sounds good."

Aaron turned to face J.D. "I admitted it, okay? Now we can do things however you want. However you want to settle this between us."

J.D. looked at him with a bright, happy smile.

"You are Aaron," the hulking student said. He didn't sound the least bit like J.D. "Judgment Day" Harms.

Aaron stumbled back.

"Is that right?" the student before him asked. "Aahhr-ronn?"

He sounded as if he wasn't sure how to form words with a human tongue.

"You're not him," Aaron said.

The figure before him stretched out his hand.

"Him? Who?" the figure asked. "I am me."

"Oh, man," Aaron whispered.

Then there was shuffling in the halls, running footsteps. Bertram and Claire raced into the room from opposite directions.

"Everybody is waking up," Bertram said. "No dinosaurs. No damage to the school. No one seems to have a clue what really happened."

"Except us," Claire said.

Aaron watched as Bertram raced to the window.

"Look," Bertram said. "Everything is the way it should be."

Aaron finally noticed the bright golden sunlight streaming in, the soft blue of the sky, the trees outside, the houses across the street, and the cars sailing past.

"Everything's okay," Bertram said. "He did it. J.D.

went into the nexus and he put it all back together."

Bertram turned to the hulking figure standing next to Aaron. *"You* did it."

"Hello," the student said. "You are Berrrrt-rommm. Yes?"

Bertram and Aaron exchanged glances.

"It's not J.D.," Aaron said.

"Oh, but it is," the young student said. He held out a huge, meaty hand. "I am Jae'Dee."

Aaron looked at Claire. "Be strong for me, I think I'm going to faint."

"Shut up," she said, hitting his arm. She lunged forward. "What happened to *our* J.D.?"

"He's here," Jae'Dee said.

Bertram shook his head. "You mean he's sharing that body with you?"

Jae'Dee shook his head. He threw his arms wide, as if to indicate something, and almost fell. Aaron steadied him.

"I'm not used to this," Jae'Dee said. "I have no tail to help maintain balance. I've lost my center of gravity. You must excuse me."

"What about J.D.?" Aaron said.

An otherworldly smile manifested on the human features that J.D. Harms had left behind. "He is with us in all things. He became one with the nexus. He is a part of this reality, my reality, all realities. Before he became *more*, he reached out to me. He was worried that he was unworthy of the chance before him."

"Oh, man...," Bertram said.

"I told him that he should have no doubts," Jae'Dee said. "In fact, I convinced him that he was better suited to the task ahead. He said that he wanted to make things right with his family. I was now alone. My mother had been taken by the void. My father, too. I came here so that he could move on."

Claire shook her head slowly. "He sacrificed himself for us."

"He's not gone," Jae'Dee said once again. "Balance has been restored, but there are many who were taken by the void. Many beings of all realities. I don't know if they can ever be brought back. J.D. believed that they could, and so he searches all stretches of reality to find a way. And my sense is that he is quite content at the prospect of this new life and challenge."

Jae'Dee held out his hand. "Kindness is welcome." Bertram took it. "Kindness is welcome," Jae'Dee repeated.

Bertram looked around. "What about Will? He was *in* the Dinoverse. I haven't seen him. I haven't seen Mr. London, either."

Jae'Dee looked away and studied his now human feet. "Ah, yes. That. You see—"

A wind rose up. Bertram, Aaron, and Claire looked

around as a sharp crackle of lightning circled them. Sizzling bolts of energy and two voices pounded at them from everywhere and nowhere at once.

"Bertram, this is Mr. London, I did it. I helped to guide J.D. into the machine. But now I'm somewhere else..."

"Bertram, this is Will, I'm in New York and the Big Apple is *not* friendly. I need help."

Mr. London spoke again. Aaron sensed that the teacher and student could not hear each other. They were in different times. Different places.

"Bertram, I don't even know where this is," Mr. London said. "There are dinosaurs all around. Things are a little scary. I need your help."

"Bertram, help, please," Will called.

The lightning faded and the wind died down. The echoes of the voices drifted away.

"They're in two different places," Aaron said. "Two different times. And the M.I.N.D. Machine doesn't even exist anymore."

"Ah, well," Jae'Dee said. "About that. It does exist in the Dinoverse, and there is one door leading from here to there that I left open, just in case. The way will not be easy, however."

Aaron turned to Bertram and Claire. "Well, guys, what do you think? Are you up for an adventure?"

Claire looked back at a figure standing in the doorway.

Melissa. She gazed at Jae'Dee strangely.

"I think I'm gonna be needed here," Claire said. "Jae'Dee's going to need a guide. And I don't have anything left to prove."

Aaron reached out and took her hand. "I'll come back."

She grinned. "I'll be here. Maybe we can catch a movie. You bring the pizza and the chips."

"It's a date." Aaron leaned forward, sensing that he could kiss her. She would let him.

He stepped back. There was time.

Bertram had his arms folded over his chest. "Um, hello? You're asking me if I want to see another world? Take a wild guess."

Aaron smiled. "I was just trying to be polite, bro."

Next to them, Jae'Dee described a large rectangle in the air with his hands. He stepped back, whispered something, and a blinding corridor of blue-white light appeared.

The doorway was before them.

"After you," Bertram said.

"Oh, no," Aaron replied. "After you, I insist."

Laughing, they stepped through the door together.

BERTRAM'S NOTEBOOK

Apatosaurus (uh-PAT-uh-SORE-us): The name means "deceptive lizard." Apatosaurus was a long-necked plant-eater that grew to 69 feet in length and weighed up to 24 tons. Its tail contained 82 bones and was used like a whip in defense against predators.

Apatosaurus

Archaeopteryx (ar-kee-OP-tur-iks): The name means "ancient wing." Archaeopteryx has long been considered the first bird, and it is also sometimes called a feathered dinosaur. It was two feet in length and fed on insects and small animals.

Archaeopteryx

Brontosaurus (BRON-tuh-SORE-us): The original name given to the sauropod Apatosaurus, later discarded by the scientific community. The term is still commonly used outside paleontological circles to refer to a variety of long-necks.

Carcharodontosaurus (kar-KAR-uh-DON-tuh-SORE-us): The name means "shark-toothed lizard." This dinosaur was a bipedal meat-eater with features like those of Allosaurus and Tyrannosaurus. A recently discovered specimen in this family sported an unusual and frightening scissor-shaped jaw. It was 45 feet long, 5 feet of which was skull.

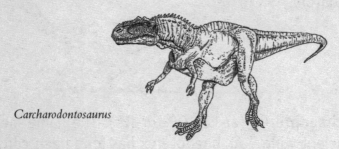

Carcharodontosaurus

Carnivores (KAR-nuh-vorz): Meat-eating animals.

Compsognathus (komp-sog-NAY-thus): The name means "elegant jaw." Compsognathus was a small meat-eater ranging from two to four feet in length. Weighing only six pounds, Compsognathus used its lightweight frame and incredible speed to catch small animals for food.

Compsognathus

Corythosaurus (kuh-RITH-uh-SORE-us): The name means "helmet lizard." One of the best-known duck-billed dinosaurs, Corythosaurus was a plant-eater that grew up to 33 feet long and had a high, hollow, bony head crest. Scientists believe that Corythosaurus could use their crests to make sounds that warned of predators and to communicate in other ways with members of their herds.

Corythosaurus

Deinonychus (die-NON-ih-kus): The name means "terrible claw." This dinosaur could be up to 10 feet long and had large fangs, a powerful jaw, muscular legs, and a retractable scythe-like claw on the second toe of each foot. Commonly known as "raptors," Deinonychus were fast and agile and usually hunted in packs to take down large prey.

Dilophosaurus (die-LOH-fuh-SORE-us): The name means "two-ridge lizard." Called "the terror of the early Jurassic," Dilophosaurus was a lithe, 19-foot-long hunter with a long tail. Two fragile semicircular crests rose from the head.

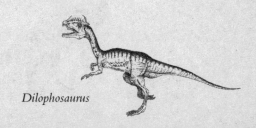

Dilophosaurus

Herbivores (HUR-bih-vorz): Plant-eating animals.

Hypsilophodon (hip-suh-LOH-fuh-don): The name means "high-ridge tooth." This dinosaur was a small herbivore, only about four to seven feet in length, but it was very quick. It walked on its two strong back legs.

Invertebrates (in-VUR-tuh-braytz): Animals without backbones, such as jellyfish.

Jurassic (juh-RAS-ik): The second of three distinct periods in the Mesozoic Era. The Jurassic Period began approximately 208 million years ago and ended 144 million years ago.

Massospondylus (mas-oh-SPON-duh-lus): The name means "massive vertebra." Massospondylus was a 16-foot-long, plant-eating dinosaur that walked on all fours and had vicious thumb claws that could be used for defense or as tools.

Massospondylus

Mesozoic Era (mez-uh-ZOH-ik ER-uh): The age of dinosaurs, 245 million to 65 million years ago.

Microvenator (MIE-kroh-vih-NAY-tor): The name means "tiny hunter." It was a small carnivorous dinosaur that walked on its hind legs and had unusually long arms.

Pachycephalosaurus (pack-ih-SEF-uh-luh-SORE-us): The name means "thick-headed lizard." These planteaters used their domelike heads for defense, ramming opponents with them much like present-day mountain goats.

Paleontologist (pay-lee-un-TAHL-uh-jist): A scientist who studies the past through fossils.

Scissor-jaw: See Carcharodontosaurus.

Scutellosaurus (skoo-TEL-uh-SORE-us): This dinosaur was named after the hundreds of scutes (bony studs) along its body, which shielded the animal from attack. It could walk or run on all fours or balance on its hind legs using its tail. This small plant-eater was four feet long.

Scutellosaurus

Stegosaurus (STEG-uh-SORE-us): The name means "roof lizard," which comes from the bony plates that jutted upward from the neck, back, and upper tail. This plant-eater grew up to 29 feet long and weighed two tons. Its main defensive weapon against attack was its tail, armed with four to eight spikes, each three to four feet long. The tail could be used with force and speed because of the dinosaur's ability to pivot very quickly on its hind legs.

Stegosaurus

Syntarsus (sin-TAR-sus): The name means "fused ankle." It was a 10-foot-long bipedal meat-eater. It was also fast-moving and had a long, flexible neck and a hollow tail.

Vertebrates (VUR-tuh-braytz): Animals with backbones, such as fish, mammals, reptiles, and birds.

The world: The continents and the seas of the earth 150 million years ago were very different from those of today. The supercontinent Pangaea was breaking up during the Jurassic Period. The Atlantic Ocean was created from rifts in the continents. Volcanic activity raged along much of what is now the west coast of the United States. Africa began to split from South America. The region that is now India prepared to drift toward Asia. Climates were warm worldwide.

The World—Present Day

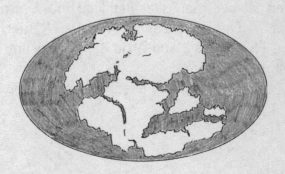

The World—150 Million Years Ago

• AUTHOR'S SPECIAL THANKS •

Thanks to Denise Ciencin, M.A., National Certified Counselor, for her many valued and wonderful contributions to this novel. For helping me to reconstruct the world of California 150 million years ago, thanks to paleontologists Richard Hilton, Professor, Department of Geology, Sierra College, Rocklin, California; Frank DeCourten, Professor, Department of Geology and Earth Sciences, Sierra College, Rocklin, California; Robert F. Walters, Paleontological Life Restoration Artist, American Museum of Natural History, New York City, New York; and Dr. Phillip J. Currie, Curator of Dinosaurs, Royal Tyrrell Museum of Palaeontology, Adjunct Associate Professor, University of Calgary, and Adjunct Professor, University of Saskatchewan, Canada.

Special thanks to Alice Alfonsi, my extraordinary editor, and all our friends at Random House, especially Kate Klimo, Cathy Goldsmith, Tanya Mauler, Mike Wortzman, Lisa Findlay, and Artie Bennett, Jenny Golub, and Christopher Shea.

Final thanks to my incredible agent, Jonathan Matson.